IN THE

'*Stop antagonising Dr Alexandre,*' Student Nurse
Anna Curtis is told. But is it Anna's fault that her
mere presence has such an adverse effect on the
normally good-humoured senior medical registrar?

IN THE NAME
OF LOVE

BY

HAZEL FISHER

MILLS & BOON LIMITED
London · Sydney · Toronto

First published in Great Britain 1983
by Mills & Boon Limited, 15–16 Brook's Mews,
London W1A 1DR

© Hazel Fisher 1983

Australian copyright 1983
Philippine copyright 1983

ISBN 0 263 74444 2

Set in 11 on 11½ pt Linotron Times
03/1083–51,000

Photoset by Rowland Phototypesetting Ltd
Bury St Edmunds, Suffolk
Made and printed in Great Britain by
Richard Clay (The Chaucer Press) Ltd
Bungay, Suffolk

CHAPTER ONE

STUDENT Nurse Anna Curtis paused uncertainly outside the ward office door. It was ajar and she heard the murmur of voices within. Trying to compose herself for the ordeal of a new ward, she heard a woman's laugh from the office, then one of the voices was raised sufficiently for her to hear.

She caught the name 'Ricky', then with a hand that trembled, knocked on the door and pushed it open. Probably it was Sister listening to the night nurse's gossip. Whoever it was they couldn't possibly eat her.

Two pairs of interested eyes were turned upon Anna and she wished, not for the first time, that she wasn't so tall and curvy with hair a riot of dark red curls, wide-spaced green eyes and the creamy, delicately lovely complexion that often went with red hair.

The emaciated-looking Staff Nurse waved Anna to a chair. 'Hello. You're the new first-year aren't you? I saw you last week.'

'Yes, Staff,' Anna said, quietly, sitting down in a corner, trying to be as unobtrusive as possible. It was her sad experience that her looks and figure caused unwarranted envy at first, until people got to know her better and realised she was quiet and unassuming and couldn't care less *how* pretty she was. So she had learned to keep a low profile. As Park was only her second ward she would be expected to be unobtrusive anyway. First-year students were the lowest form of life at St Aidan's, a medium-sized, fairly new hospital in the south, within walking distance of Anna's home.

Staff Nurse Powell peered at Anna's namebadge. 'Student Nurse A. Curtis. I'll mark you as present, then. There will be two more of us very shortly—a third-year, Pauline Wilson, and a very experienced auxiliary, Mrs Barratt. You can tag along with Mrs Barratt just for a while,' she added, and Anna, after asking if she might look down the list of patients, sat back again, leaving the other two to finish their conversation. It wasn't yet 7.30 and the other night nurse would still be in the ward.

Anna tried to concentrate on the various ailments, knowing how impossible it would be for a day or two to match up names and faces with diseases. Park was men's medical and held twenty-eight beds in the main ward plus four beds in the side-ward. The main disorder, as she had suspected, was heart trouble, but there were two diabetic men and a jaundiced patient with inoperable carcinoma. The ward was full except for the side-room, and likely to remain so, she mused. Then she found herself inadvertently listening to the conversation instead of concentrating on the list.

'I thought at first his eyes were dark blue,' the night nurse was saying, 'but I think they're really *grey*-blue.'

'They are,' Staff Nurse affirmed. 'He has a devastatingly sad spaniel look,' she giggled. 'That direct blue-grey gaze is very fetching. Particularly when he's been told he can't have something he wants, like when Sister told him he couldn't borrow the auxiliary for something or other. He looked really hurt, and his eyes went all moist and soulful, like my dog when I've forgotten it's time for walkies!'

Anna's lips twitched. Presumably this soulful-eyed spaniel type was the house doctor. He sounded fascinating.

Voices and footsteps approached and the rest of the morning shift arrived. Anna knew Pauline Wilson by sight. She was a pleasant brunette of around Anna's own age, which was just twenty-one. The auxiliary, Mrs Barratt, was about forty-five, she judged. Thank goodness she was experienced. Sometimes first-years were left to follow other newcomers, picking up knowledge as best they could—and picking up bad habits at the same time.

The night nurse ran quickly through the list of patients, reading out the relevant information from the Kardex, and Anna listened intently, rapidly making notes of jobs to be carried out, just as the others were doing.

'There. That's it, Staff. The only real problem is Mr Graham. Dr Smith will be along to see him later. Or the Jerseyman, perhaps!' The night nurse had a pleasant, tinkling laugh, and Staff Nurse Powell giggled.

'Our Ricky Jerseyman might come, especially as Dr Tester is sick.' Turning to Anna, she explained: 'Ricky Jerseyman is Dr Alexandre, the senior medical registrar. Dr Tester, the consultant, is sick and old Dr Smith is standing in for him, but Dr Alexandre does most of the work.'

'Why Ricky Jerseyman?' Anna wanted to know. 'It makes him sound like a potato!'

Staff Nurse snorted, displeased at the laughter that greeted Anna's remark, and Anna mentally slapped herself. She hadn't been unobtrusive for long enough.

'He's from the Channel Islands. Jersey, I believe,' Staff Nurse said crisply, standing up and adjusting her belt so that the ornate silver buckle gleamed in the light.

They all trooped into the ward to begin the day's work. Being a medical ward it was heavy going but perhaps less so than women's medical, Coppice Ward. The men tended not to be so overweight as the women, according to Mrs Barratt, who was a cheerful mine of information.

'All the wards are arranged on similar lines, love,' she explained as they walked along the row of beds, Anna shyly greeting each patient as they passed, aware of the hubbub her arrival had caused.

'You're a nice armful, dear!' one of the patients called and Anna coloured, wishing she could sink through the floor.

'Get noticed more, you being a redhead,' the auxiliary commented. 'Shouldn't worry about them. They're good sorts. Mind your bottom when they are nearly ready for discharge, though!'

The ward was compact, with the sluice and bathrooms at one end, a nurses' station in the middle of the ward, and treatment room, linen-cupboard and kitchen at the other.

'The nurses' station is usually staffed,' Ruth Barratt explained, 'but as we're dodging about most of the morning we can see if anything goes wrong.'

After the pressure of a surgical ward, medical

seemed slow-moving. With no patients to be readied for surgery, Anna found they had more time to chat to the men, though they had to work while they talked. She had imagined medical to be a hard slog and so it was, in a way, with urinals, back trolleys, bed-making, lifting—but the atmosphere was more relaxed. Patients tended to stay longer for one thing, sometimes several weeks, and they gave the ward more character.

Mrs Barratt said she thought of the patients as one big happy family, and gradually Anna came to see what she meant. But on this first morning she had to concentrate mainly on picking up the routine.

Ruth Barratt greeted each man by name as they worked, which helped Anna considerably. After breakfast most of the men would dress and sit in the small day-room, and Anna decided this would be the best chance to get to know those few who remained in bed.

Giving out breakfasts was an ordeal, with Staff Nurse merely making gestures in an approximate direction. Anna had to glance at the names over the beds in case she made a mistake, though Ruth Barratt helped as much as she could. Two patients required help with eating and Anna was delegated to one of them, a Mr Cumming.

Mr Cumming was a short, portly man with a military moustache and a cheerful grin. He was also newly-blinded in a works accident and required supervision and explanation at meal times, though he liked to place the food in his mouth himself.

Anna explained who she was and what he was having for breakfast. 'Aha! A new voice. What are

you like, my love?' he asked. 'A gorgeous redhead
or a beautiful blonde?'

'Neither. The fish is on your fork, Mr Cumming,'
Anna said firmly.

He chewed steadily, though the fish was so tender he could have swallowed without chewing.
'You can't be bald!' he guffawed, and Anna tried to
quieten him.

'Please! Don't get excited, Mr Cumming. I'm a
redhead. Dark red actually,' she told him, hoping
the matter would be dropped, because she saw
Staff Nurse glance sharply over at them.

But the patient insisted on knowing her general
shape, as well as the colour of her eyes, and her
Christian name. She could imagine how much details of that nature would mean to a man who had
become blind in his middle years, so she supplied
the relevant information, gently teasing him all the
while.

'Best breakfast I've had for years, Nurse darling,' he assured her as she stacked the dishes. He
put out a large, work-roughened hand, as if to
reassure himself she was still there, and before she
could stop him he knocked the tray to the ground
with a resounding crash.

Anna put her hands up to her face in horror, then
hurriedly comforted the patient, who kept apolo-
gising. Her face was as red as her hair, and she
heard the sound of crepe-soled shoes approaching.
Staff Nurse Powell would *not* be amused.

Turning quickly, she bumped into the owner of
the crepe-soled shoes—a tall, dark-haired man in a
white coat. A tall dark-haired man with a very
angry expression—and big blue-grey eyes.

Words of apology trembled on her lips but were ignored as the white-coated man spoke to Mr Cumming.

'Dr Alexandre, Mr Cumming. Welfare have found you a place. Near Southampton. Will that do for you? Not too far from your son.' His voice was gentle, concerned, and Anna forgot her embarrassment and, at a gesture from Staff Nurse, she swept up the broken crockery, trying to avoid Dr Alexandre's feet.

He had large feet, shod in tan suede shoes. She had time to notice only that before she scurried away with the crockery in a dustpan, leaving the hastily-summoned domestic to clear the rest once the doctor had finished.

'How could you be so careless!' Staff Nurse flared, as Anna obeyed the beckoning finger and presented herself at the office. 'You know many of these patients have heart disease and need keeping quiet! Being a first-year doesn't excuse carelessness, Nurse.'

'No, Staff. I'm sorry. I'm very sorry,' Anna added, which was true. Although the fault was not hers, not only had the noise upset the ward, it had upset Dr Alexandre. He of the blue-grey eyes and sad spaniel look.

She hadn't had time to notice any sad spaniel expression, but perhaps it would come later. At least she hadn't upset a consultant—yet.

After breakfasts were cleared away and Staff Nurse had seen to the doctor, she offered to run through the list of patients with Anna, who hoped she would be able to memorise the information.

'Park Ward is a twenty-eight bedder, then we

have the side-ward, as you've seen,' Staff Nurse began. 'At the moment we haven't any patients there because women's medical are using it. They're over the top and haven't a vacancy anywhere so we'll just have to manage somehow if we get another admission.'

Staff Nurse sighed and ran long fingers through her short fair hair. 'Sister will be on tomorrow so that's a relief. She can deal with Dr Smith, who's rather a pain. He's the consultant standing in for Paul Tester, who's sick,' she explained. 'A few of the patients belong to Dr Carter—he does a round on Wednesday.' Then she began on the patients, explaining each disorder briefly.

Whatever Staff Nurse Powell lacked on the personality side, Anna was forced to admit that she knew her job. She obviously enjoyed teaching too, and some of the dread left her. Things weren't as bad as she'd expected. Why, she might even be able to eat some lunch! She'd been so fearful that morning that she couldn't even manage a cup of coffee, and she knew her stomach would soon start protesting.

'Mr Cumming is, as you know, blind,' Staff Nurse was saying. 'But that isn't why he's in a medical ward, of course. Did he tell you what was wrong with him?' Grey eyes homed in on Anna, who was pleased to be able to say she knew.

'He didn't tell me, but I was looking at the list earlier, Staff Nurse, and I remembered because he was the only blind patient. He had quite severe hypertension but he's almost cured now.'

Staff Nurse frowned. 'I wouldn't say cured, but he's a good deal better. Certainly if he takes things easy he should be all right, and Rick, I mean Dr Alexandre, has fixed up for him to go into a home. There is no one at his home to tend to him,' she finished sadly, and Anna sighed.

'He seems such a dear,' she said wistfully, 'and he was very apologetic about his accident with the breakfast dishes. He . . .'

'Accident? Do you mean the breakage was *his* fault?' Staff Nurse shot at her, and Anna hesitated before nodding.

'He couldn't help it, Staff. Really.' Worry caused her to frown. Surely he wouldn't have to pay for the broken crockery?'

'Why ever didn't you say so before? I wouldn't have ticked you off,' Staff Nurse went on wryly. 'Never take the blame for something you didn't do. First-years get blamed enough as it is. Then we have Mr Graham,' she continued. 'He isn't too well this morning and Dr Alexandre had a look at him. Personally I think it's all in the mind. He has a vivid imagination and might worry himself into a gastric ulcer. His heart isn't too good, though. Any questions so far?'

'Only about the type of patient, Staff. Do you get much variety of disorder?' Anna ventured. 'I mean, most of them are heart trouble. Only three have something else.'

'Yes, but heart trouble can cover a variety of things, Nurse,' Staff Nurse sighed. 'It isn't just *one* condition. But generally speaking we do get mainly coronaries. We get a lot of patients from ITU once their condition is more stable. We've got an admission from there, probably tomorrow.' She checked the admission book. 'He'll have to take Mr Excell's bed. He's the inoperable carcinoma,' she added.

Anna had met Mr Excell briefly at breakfast, a tall, yellow-skinned man. 'He's going home then?' she queried, and Staff Nurse shrugged.

'What else is there to do with him? He isn't quite at death's door yet. Anyway, there isn't any terminal care home he can go to, so we're discharging him to his wife. She's willing to nurse him. You could pack his belongings for him after breakfast tomorrow. Better make a note of that.'

Anna began to write but Staff Nurse stopped her. 'No wait. Better let Ruth Barratt do it. He knows her well and he might not like a stranger helping him.'

Anna beamed. Staff Nurse Powell had gone up considerably in her estimation, showing she cared about the feelings of a dying patient.

'There. That's it, I think. Did you do injections on your other ward?'

'Only one, Staff Nurse. It was rather an ordeal,' Anna confessed, and Staff Nurse smiled sympathetically.

'It still is, as far as I'm concerned, Nurse Curtis. I hate giving them! Did you do last offices at all? I suppose not.'

'No, I didn't. I expect you get a lot here?' Anna ventured. She had never seen a dead person and wasn't sure she could cope.

'Not that many. It just depends. I hope you enjoy Park Ward, anyway. You live in, I suppose?'

Anna shook her head. 'No, I'm local.'

'Oh? So am I. I've a flat now but my parents live in Green Street. Where do you live?'

Anna hesitated but really had no option. 'Oh, a

bit nearer than that. At the bottom of Brightling Hill.'

'*Do* you?' Staff Nurse leaned forward, eyes widening in astonishment. 'They're big houses, aren't they? Surely you don't have one of those mansions?'

'Well, not exactly,' Anna admitted, and Staff Nurse looked relieved.

'You've a flat then. Some of them *are* divided, now I think of it. I was going to say if you had the whole house you wouldn't need to work!'

Anna smiled, bitterly. I *do* have the whole house! she wanted to yell. And I *don't* need to work! I took a job so that I could escape for a few hours every day.

If only Staff Nurse knew! Being shut up in one of those creepy old houses with an ailing mother and a couple of middle-aged women was no joke. Not that Anna begrudged helping to care for her mother, of course. Indeed, the knowledge that she was gaining as a nurse would benefit her. That was probably the reason her mother hadn't created too much of a fuss when Anna had insisted on doing the nurse training.

The rest of the morning passed swiftly without Anna doing anything terribly wrong and she began to grow in confidence. That such a big girl should be nervous and lacking in self-confidence might seem odd to others, Anna mused as she hurried to the canteen. But her upbringing had done nothing to prepare her to take her place as a leader. She had been kept firmly under her mother's thumb, even before the coronary attack which led to Mrs Curtis becoming an invalid, virtually a recluse, too.

'Hello Anna! How's the new ward?' Bryan Harris, one of only two boys in her set asked as they queued together in the canteen.

'Interesting. I think I might like it,' Anna conceded. 'It's a job remembering names, though.'

He nodded, then waved to one of the other girls, Shirley Weston, a neat little blonde. 'See you, Anna.'

'Yes, sure,' she murmured, choosing a small corner table. Being two or three years older than most of the set was rather a bind. Sometimes she felt years older, not just twenty-one. It made it difficult for her to form friendships, though there was a girl of about twenty-three in the set, Sheila Haggerty. Even she seemed more at ease with the others than Anna did, and a sigh escaped her as she gazed around the small canteen.

Groups of laughing, chattering learners were everywhere. The higher-ups had to use the canteen as well—no consultants' dining-rooms here. Anna noticed Dr Wilmott, their house doctor, with several others in white coats, bleeps clipped to the front of their breast-pockets. She couldn't see Ricky Jerseyman, though!

'Mind if I join you?' Suzie Almazan, a Filipino second-year, sat down and smiled at Anna, who felt the years and the worries roll off her. It was good to be a nurse and good to have someone to talk to.

She hummed a little tune as she strolled back to the ward, trying not to feel self-conscious. Everyone had the national uniform of plain white dress. First-year students wore a white belt to denote their lowly status, together with a butterfly cap – a horror of starched linen dreamed up by someone who hated nurses, Anna thought. It was becoming but the very devil to make up, particularly when fresh from the laundry.

Unfortunately, the white dress was rather tight and accentuated her full figure. Her large rounded breasts were eye-catching, as she'd found out, and she longed to hide behind a starched apron!

The afternoon shift had arrived on duty when Anna returned. One of them was male, Albert Grainger, an auxiliary. Staff Nurse had told her they ought to have a male nurse on each shift but that 'flu had knocked them down and it might be a week or two before they got another male student. They could, in any case, always borrow a male nurse for any intimate procedure.

Albert, a friendly West Indian, beamed at Anna then whistled appreciatively as she hovered in the office doorway.

She was about to ask for Staff Nurse when a cool voice spoke from behind, 'Do you *have* to block the doorway, Nurse?' Dr Alexandre none too gently moved her to one side by placing his hands around her waist and lifting.

She could not suppress the blush that suffused her face and neck, and Dr Alexandre chuckled. 'A nurse who blushes! What will they think of next? Get me Mr Gabriel's notes.'

'I beg your pardon?' Anna had never heard of Mr Gabriel and didn't think they had a patient of that name.

'Mr Gabriel's notes,' the registrar repeated, very slowly, and Anna flushed even more. 'His notes. I want them, Nurse!' Those blue-grey eyes were fixed on Anna as she hurried to the filing cabinet and began flicking through the folders.

Fortunately Albert came to her rescue. 'Here they are, Doctor!' Anna whirled around. Albert was holding them aloft and he grinned at her.

'They were on the desk, honey. He's coming in tomorrow.'

'He is indeed, Albert. Thanks,' Dr Alexandre said, shooting Anna an irritated look. 'If you can't be bothered to learn anything Nurse, may I suggest you look elsewhere for employment?'

Outraged at the injustice of his remark, Anna was about to protest but the registrar continued, relentlessly. 'I suppose, being beautiful, you spend all your time preening in front of a mirror instead of attending to your patients. Now, for God's sake get out and find something to do!' he finished cuttingly, his mouth a hard slit, lines of temper showing on his rugged, forceful face.

Albert rolled his eyes in mock horror. 'Come on, Nurse. 'I'll find you something to do.' Anna allowed herself to be led from the office just as Staff Nurse Powell came back.

She heard Dr Alexandre's voice as she followed the auxiliary. 'You'll have to get a bigger office, Staff Nurse. Or a smaller student! That one keeps getting in the way!' Staff Nurse's distinctive giggle was all Anna heard as she marched away, head held proudly, tears not far away.

How could they be so unkind? She bit her lower lip until it hurt, then a patient called her over and she forgot her own troubles. One thing was for sure, Dr Alexandre was no sad, wistful-eyed spaniel, he was a fierce alsatian with sharp teeth and snapping jaws!

None too soon four-thirty came round and Anna went to the office to ask permission to leave. It had been a very long, tiring day and an upsetting one, too.

Staff Nurse grunted her permission, then reminded Anna that Sister would be on duty the next day.

Anna hesitantly asked what Sister Noakes was like to work for, and Staff Nurse Powell raised a pencilled brow. 'Let's put it this way—if she's had a bad weekend, we will all suffer for it!'

A crestfallen Anna walked through the ward door, wishing she hadn't asked. Today had been bad enough but what would tomorrow be like? If she had any more brushes with the senior registrar, she wasn't sure she would last long on Park Ward. Hopefully, the consultants wouldn't notice her. They never seemed to recognise students or any form of nursing life under SEN or Staff Nurse, so that was something to be grateful for.

Dr Smith, the locum consultant, she'd already met briefly. He was semi-retired with a bark worse than his bite. Dr Carter she knew nothing about so she must meet that challenge when it arose. Dr Paul Tester she knew by reputation. He was a bit of a rake, by all accounts, but a good doctor. Anna snuggled further into her sheepskin jacket, the bitter December air hitting her as she hurried down the hospital drive. Dr Tester was also dynamic, or so she'd heard, a forceful personality who steam-rollered people into doing things his way whether they wanted to or not. Rather like Dr Alexandre, she mused.

That man! She refused to think about the doctor

from the Channel Islands. But she couldn't keep him out of her mind for long. He was rude, arrogant, boorish, and dreadfully unkind. He had no right to make that remark about her being too big for the office! She was only five feet eight—he was much taller, with wide shoulders that almost filled the doorway.

Anna clenched her fists inside her woollen gloves. Once she was trained she would make him eat his words! There was nothing attractive about the man and his personality was nil as far as she was concerned. She couldn't think what the night nurse and Staff Nurse Powell found to eulogise about.

Home was some twenty minutes' walk, across the recreation ground and along a dimly-lit lane. They were, as she'd told Staff Nurse, at the bottom of Brightling Hill, so she didn't have to face a tiring climb at the end of a busy day.

How would Mother be? she wondered. She was always more difficult when Anna returned to duty after days off. She was desperately lonely and Anna wished she would invite friends in as she used to. Unfortunately, her mother was convinced that one coronary meant she had to lead an invalid's life, something Anna felt wasn't good for her. In her reading on heart disorders she had discovered that once the lesion was healed a little gentle activity was beneficial, indeed essential, and she was determined to persuade her mother to live a little more. The persuasion would have to be gentle and prolonged but Anna believed that her mother would eventually agree. It would just take time and patience. Last year she had roused herself sufficiently to spend a few days in Bournemouth but it hadn't been a success.

A sudden movement by the hedge caught her eye, and she jumped. A fox, perhaps? Or Jasper, the cat? Or . . .

A shape materialised from the darkness and Anna opened her mouth to scream.

'Anna! It's me!' a hoarse voice whispered, and relief shot through her.

'Mike! Oh, Mike!' Then she was in his arms and the frustrations and worries of the day rolled away. Nothing else mattered.

'Thought you weren't coming, Anna. I've been here hours. It feels like hours, anyway,' Mike Forster chuckled, taking her by the hand and walking back the way she'd come.

'I mustn't be long, Mike. Mother will worry and phone the hospital if I'm not home by five,' Anna said, worry flooding back.

'That mother of yours has too much of her own way!' Mike exploded, and when Anna opened her mouth to protest, he kissed her again.

It was a lingering kiss and she trembled, desire mounting and overshadowing her concern for her mother. She loved him! It was so unfair having to meet like this, as though they were cheating on a marriage partner, slinking from one assignation to the next. They loved each other and there was no reason for them not to marry.

If marriage was what Mike had in mind, a cautionary voice whispered. Anyway, the voice persisted, it could kill Mother. What if she guessed?

With a sigh, Anna broke away and put a hand up

to her throbbing head. If Mother knew she would make a scene and that could be fatal. 'Oh, Mike!' Anna said, dazedly, looking to him for comfort.

It was dark and overcast and they had to keep away from the street light, so all she could see of him was his height, little more than hers, and the outline of his shaggy head. As always he needed a haircut and Anna was overcome with tenderness and love for him.

But when he moved to take her into his arms again, she resisted. 'I have to go in, Mike. They will be waiting tea for me.'

'Yeah, all right. But listen. I've got some good news. Wait till you hear!' he chuckled, and her heart lifted.

Perhaps he was going to say that their relationship could come out into the open now, that he'd found a way of declaring his love without upsetting her mother! She waited, breathlessly.

CHAPTER TWO

'I'VE found a new flat—in Shipley Street,' Mike said smugly, and disappointment stabbed at Anna.

'That's wonderful, Mike. Will you still share with the other boys?'

'No, that's the great thing. I'll be on my own— and it's near the hospital so you can meet me there at dinner times!' he said triumphantly. Before Anna could protest, he took her into his arms again and they clung together, desperation lending a poignancy to their embrace.

It was so unfair that they had to meet furtively like this! 'I . . . I have to go, Mike. Good luck with your new flat,' Anna said quietly, pulling herself free and beginning to walk away.

'Hey! Wait, Anna!' Mike caught up with her and forced her to stop. 'I thought you'd be pleased! We can get really cosy during your meal break. Why, you could cook us a nice meal. Be like being married, it would,' he coaxed, and Anna wavered.

'Perhaps. I'll pop round to see the flat once you're settled in, then we'll see,' she conceded, and Mike patted her cheek.

'That's my girl! See you.'

She listened to his receding footsteps, her anxious eyes following his dimly visible shape until it disappeared completely. She almost sobbed in her anguish and frustration, then placed her hand over her heart where she kept a tiny photo of Mike in a locket hung from a slender gold chain. A locket and a photograph about which her mother knew nothing.

They had waited tea for her, as always, and she felt ashamed. They were good to her, all three of them, and she was a selfish girl to want more from life.

Her mother, Jennifer, was only in her late forties, a tall, buxom woman, though she was thinner than she used to be. Anna had inherited her dark red hair as well as her shape. Only the big green eyes came from her late father, a professor, who'd been killed six years before.

Jennifer missed him still and sometimes spoke of seeing him sitting in his favourite chair in the study.

The other two females in the household were Mary Dixon, Mother's nurse, and Mrs Jenkins, the cook-housekeeper. In addition they had a daily woman, Mrs Walker, to do the rough work, and a twice-weekly gardener, a crabby old man who did odd-jobs during the winter months. Apart from occasional visits from the doctor, the gardener, Mr Hill, was the only man Anna ever saw except for the staff and patients at St Aidan's. And Mike, of course.

'Anna! You're late, dear,' her mother said anxiously, and Anna hurried forward to kiss her. Jennifer stroked her daughter's cheek, just as Mike had done earlier, and Anna flinched, feeling more ashamed than ever.

'Anna, whatever is it? Have you had a bad day? Go and wash and change out of that tight dress and tell me about the ward,' she commanded, and Anna did as she was bid.

Mrs Curtis was always interested in the goings-on at the hospital and, once she'd got over the shock of hearing that Anna was going to be a nurse, she'd seemed pleased. All in all, mother and daughter got on well together, and Anna was learning how to cope with her mother's possessiveness—but this business of Mike . . . How would her mother view that?

She stripped down to her sensible underwear, the locket gleaming brightly between her breasts. Lovingly she fingered it, snapping it open to have one quick gaze at Mike Forster.

He was dark-haired, and his hair was crinkly and springy, full of life when Anna ran her fingers through it. His pale blue eyes gazed steadfastly at her from the photo. Anna felt they were brimming with love. Or was it simply laughter? Her fingers closed convulsively about the locket before she hurried to the bathroom.

Mike Forster was the only secret she kept from her mother. They had met the previous summer at Bournemouth. Mary and Anna between them had managed to persuade Jennifer to take the holiday and Bournemouth wasn't too far away. It wasn't Anna's idea of a dynamic holiday venue, being an area popular for retirement with a seafront full of ladies in the winter of their lives, but it was peaceful early in the season and Anna had managed to get out on her own quite a bit.

On one of her solitary walks Mike had come up to ask her for a light, though he admitted afterwards that he didn't need one.

The unsophisticated Anna had been thrilled that a boy as attractive as Mike, with his crinkly hair, pleasant, almost handsome face and splendid physique, should be interested, and the relationship had snowballed, particularly when she found that Mike also lived in Middleborough, sharing a flat with five others.

There was nothing sexual in their relationship—yet. But Anna yearned to belong to him, for she loved him and was sure he loved her. It wouldn't be a casual one night stand affair, she was convinced. They were in love and oh, how she longed to tell the world! She wanted to shout from the rooftops, proclaim that she loved Mike Forster and would deny him nothing.

But she wanted to be married. She wanted to spend the rest of her life with Mike, but wondered if his love would extend to that. Marriage was a tie for a man. She could see that, could understand his reluctance. He was only twenty-three and she knew girls matured emotionally sooner than boys, and she was mature for her age.

Perhaps in time he would come to see things her way, she reasoned, as she ran lightly down stairs, her full grey skirt swirling about her long, slender legs. Everything would come, in time.

'You, Nurse!'

Anna whirled round, nearly losing her hateful cap in the process. One of the grips was always working loose. The owner of the imperious voice caught up with her as she struggled with the starched cap.

'Yes, Doctor,' she said quietly, wishing Dr Alexandre miles away.

A smile touched his mouth then was gone, and

Anna thought she must have imagined it. 'Here, let me.' He took the grips from Anna's cold fingers, set the butterfly cap on at its proper angle, then pushed the grips firmly into place.

He stood back to admire his handiwork, eyes serious, and Anna could feel herself blushing.

'Yes. That will do, I think. A neat job if I say so myself,' he said smugly, and Anna bit her tongue to stop herself from snapping at him.

'Thank you, Doctor,' she said instead, then waited, supposing he wanted to send her on some errand.

Much as she disliked his arrogant, self-satisfied manner, she had to admit he had lovely eyes. That direct look was disconcerting but exciting, too.

She began to fidget when he didn't speak. He seemed to be memorising her face, though surely with her height and red hair she stood out enough?

'I have to apologise,' he said softly, and she opened her mouth in surprise then closed it again. 'For ticking you off for not knowing Mr Gabriel was being admitted today,' he explained, seeing the puzzlement in her clear green eyes.

'Oh! That. I'd forgotten, Doctor. Really,' she assured him blandly, secretly pleased that he realised she was new on Park Ward.

'Being new myself I didn't realise yesterday was your first day on the ward.' He smiled then, actually smiled, and Anna's lovely eyes crinkled with laughter in response, her face alight.

Smiling back at the senior registrar was evidently not the done thing and his face closed up, his aquiline nostrils flaring. Anna's smile faded. With a polite 'Thank you again, Doctor,' she hurried on towards Park Ward, crestfallen without quite knowing why.

Whatever she did would be wrong for that man, she thought crossly. She could hear the clatter of dishes as she hurried through the ward doors. She was on late shift today so would not have the whole day with Sister, who probably went off duty at five.

She was early and only Sister was in the office, busily writing in the Kardex. Sister looked up before Anna had time to knock. She was much younger than Anna had imagined, probably in her late twenties, with elegantly coiffured black hair and heavily made-up brown eyes. *Cold* brown eyes, Anna noticed with a sinking heart. Evidently Sister's weekend had not been a successful one.

'I'm student nurse Anna Curtis, Sister,' Anna said softly, trying not to smile and possibly annoy the older woman.

Sister Noakes frowned. 'Oh, yes. Staff mentioned you. Said you kept getting in Dr Alexandre's way.'

Anna gasped. 'Only once, Sister. Anyway, he came up so quietly I didn't know he was there,' she protested, and Sister gave her a sharp look then shrugged, her scarlet mouth turning down at the corners.

'Please see that the registrar doesn't make a habit of creeping up on you. Running this ward is difficult enough without upsetting him. He's new and doesn't understand St Aidan's ways yet. I shall have to educate him,' she added smugly, and Anna decided she didn't like Sister Noakes very much.

However, ward sisters were a law unto themselves so Anna would have to do her best to get on with the woman. She only hoped Sister didn't fancy Dr Alexandre. That would make matters much worse. Though Sister wore a wedding ring, Anna mused, having been told to run along and find the SEN.

State Enrolled Nurse Hatcher, a Mauritian, was talking to one of the patients and Anna hovered uncertainly. It was the patient who saw her first, Mr Pearson, a miserable complaining little man for whom nothing was ever right. Anna had already fallen foul of him for not being quick enough to bring him fresh water.

'Yes? You're the new first-year?' the pretty SEN asked with a smile, and Anna brightened. A friendly face at last.

'She was here yesterday, Nurse. Proper slow she is,' Mr Pearson grumbled, but Nurse Hatcher only smiled, and patted his hand.

'Come along then, Nurse . . . ? What is your name?'

'Nurse Curtis. Anna Curtis, Nurse Hatcher.'

'Call me Reshma. All this Nurse this and Nurse that business is so formal,' Nurse Hatcher laughed. 'You can help me with Mr Wendlesham. He's allowed up for one hour this afternoon,' she added, as they approached the end bed.

Anna hesitated, recalling Mr Wendlesham from the day before. He was one of those bottom-pinchers Ruth Barratt had warned her about!

'After we get him up I shall go to lunch, as I am here since seven-thirty, then you will have to listen to the hand-over,' Reshma Hatcher said quietly, as they approached Mr Wendlesham.

'We have come to get you up, Mr Wendlesham,'

Reshma said firmly as the patient was about to protest. Briskly, she drew the curtains around the bed and she and Anna helped him into his dressing-gown then eased him gently into the armchair which the SEN had placed ready.

'There. Isn't it better to sit up?' Reshma asked, tucking a rug around him.

Mr Wendlesham grunted, his bold black eyes fixed on Anna who froze under the scrutiny. He was certainly on the road to recovery if he was taking an interest in women again, so Anna tried to be pleased for him. He insisted on staying by his bed rather than joining several of the others in the day-room, so they didn't try to persuade him.

'He is a bit of a loner,' Reshma warned. 'He needs supervision, that one. If he isn't watched, he will very likely try to stand up and Sister says only one hour sitting quietly in his chair. Her word is law,' Reshma added, and Anna smiled.

'I'd worked that out for myself!' she agreed.

Leaving Ruth Barratt to watch over the patients, Reshma disappeared in the direction of the canteen after calling out to Sister that she was leaving the ward.

Anna thoughtfully made her way to the office, then saw a nurse beckoning from the doorway. She quickened her pace, wondering if there was an emergency, to find Sister scowling and the others shuffling their feet uncomfortably.

'Time is of the essence, Nurse! Haven't you learned to hurry yet? I'm waiting to give the report to the afternoon shift and I can't wait about for you!'

Anna apologised gracefully, knowing quite well that she wasn't at fault, and the report began.

'You—Nurse Sulu!' Sister snapped, pointing to the African second-year, Eliza Sulu. 'This man who is coming tomorrow—Mr Snowden. He's on a cyto-toxic drug. What is that?'

Anna listened with interest, glad that Sister was keen on teaching even if her manner *was* abrupt.

Eliza hesitated and Anna longed to prompt her, but knew that wouldn't go down well. 'It's some-thing to do with cancer, Sister,' she said at last and Sister let out an exaggerated sigh.

'Obviously it has to do with cancer, since I've already told you he has that disease. *What* has it to do with cancer, Nurse Sulu?'

Eliza apparently didn't know any more, and it was Pauline Wilson who supplied the information that it was a cell-killing drug.

'It kills all cells nearby, Sister, normal cells as well as abnormal,' she said, and Sister nodded.

'Good. By Thursday, Nurse Sulu, I want a note of all the cytotoxic drugs you can find plus a discus-sion of their usefulness or otherwise,' she said firmly, and Eliza began to protest. Anna held her breath, wondering at the second-year's audacity.

'I already have two nursing-care studies to write on your patients, Sister,' Eliza said obstinately. 'And I have only four more weeks here.'

'Then I suggest you make better use of your last four weeks here than you did of the first eight!' Sister said, bitingly. Then she turned to Anna. 'As this is your second ward, I shall expect some work from you, Nurse Curtis. Read up all you can about heart disease—particularly coronaries—and set it down for me. I'll give you three weeks since you're new,' she added generously, and Anna let out her breath in relief. She had expected to be given just a couple of days like poor Eliza.

After the report, Anna followed Eliza out—just in time to see Mr Wendlesham stand up.

The auxiliary was nowhere to be seen, so Anna hurried down to the patient and told him, very firmly, to sit down.

No doubt surprised at her vehemence, he did so, a big grin on his face.

'Just testing my legs, Nurse. See if they are still working, like,' he assured her, and she smiled back.

'It was worth a try, Mr Wendlesham, but Sister will have me hung drawn and quartered if you don't behave!' she said lightly, then almost bumped into Eliza as she turned.

'Sorry, Eliza. Did you want me to help you with something?'

Eliza shrugged, lines of ill-humour on her face. 'I'm not doing much. I'll talk to Mr Wendlesham while you tidy the beds,' she said, perching herself on the bed, and Anna, eyebrows raised, went in search of Ruth Barratt.

Eliza was right when she said she wasn't doing much, for Anna and Ruth found they were slaving away all afternoon. Reshma went off at four-thirty and Sister at five, leaving Staff Nurse Powell in charge. She was doing a split duty and wasn't too happy about it.

Anna knew learners were not expected to do split shifts until they were in their third year, and only rarely then, so she had been surprised when

Sister Noakes told her she would have to do one the following day.

'Dr Carter will be doing his round in the morning,' Sister explained, 'then Dr Tester will be coming around with the senior registrar some time in the afternoon, so I need experienced staff then. He's been on sick leave, still is really, but he's keen to keep up to date with his patients.'

Anna thought in the circumstances it was a reasonable request, though her mother probably would not. She already complained when Anna had to work a late shift, which meant she didn't get home until ten. A split duty involved being at the hospital from seven-thirty until lunch, then back again at five until nine-thirty.

She could read to Mother during the afternoon break, though. That always put her in a good mood. Being off in the afternoon meant she would miss Dr Alexandre's round, and the thought irritated her—but she didn't like the man so she ought to be *glad* she would miss him, not sorry.

Feeling sad without knowing why, she went to the canteen for her tea-break—twenty minutes worth of stale sandwiches or cake and a cup of tea.

It was warm and cosy in the canteen and it was nearly empty so Anna chose a table by the window. From where she sat she could see the raindrops trailing down the windows, hear the faint patter as they hit the glass. A walk home in that would not be fun. When her father was alive they had had a car and Anna wished she could have driving lessons. Her mother could well afford another car and it would be safer for Anna when she was on night duty. Walking across a deserted recreation ground on dark nights wasn't a prospect she relished.

Yet if she pointed that out to her mother it would upset and frighten her—so much so that she would probably forbid Anna to continue at the hospital. She sighed, then stared down at the flecks of tea swimming on the surface of her cup. A teabag must have burst again.

'Is the tea not to your liking?' an amused voice asked, and Dr Alexandre drew out the chair opposite her and sat down. He needed plenty of room for his long legs just as Anna did, and inevitably their knees touched, but he seemed unaware of it.

Anna was aware, though. She could feel his warmth, and *frissons* of excitement shot along her legs then through her whole body. Gently, she shifted in her chair, and tucked her legs underneath it, trying to appear unconcerned at the same time.

Those blue-grey eyes glinted with amusement, and a warm tide of colour suffused Anna's face and neck.

The registrar watched her with interest so Anna blushed more, feeling like a specimen being examined under a powerful microscope.

'Excuse me, I have to get back,' she choked out, unsuccessfully trying to disentangle her legs from those of both the chair *and* the doctor.

When she would have fallen, the registrar gripped her upper arm, steadying her against his body. 'Are you usually so clumsy—or it is my fault?' he enquired good-humouredly. Anna tried to match his bantering tone.

'I think it must be the weather, Doctor. Only a duck would feel at home out there!'

He chuckled, his eyes crinkling with laughter, big white teeth gleaming in his tanned face. She wondered, inconsequentially, where he had got a tan like that in December. Perhaps he went somewhere more exciting for his holidays than Bournemouth!

'Have you far to walk?' he asked, still standing by the table, his tea rapidly cooling in front of him.

She shook her head. 'Not far, Doctor. Only . . .' She had been about to say 'Brightling Hill' but thought better of it. 'I have to get back to Park Ward,' she said instead, but now he was frowning.

'Where did you say you lived?' he demanded and reluctantly she told him, expecting some remark about her being one of the idle rich if she lived there.

'Hm. I know the area. Old houses—and a dark lane,' he added. Anna relaxed.

'I take a short-cut across the rec, Doctor. It cuts off most of the lane.'

'In the dark? Aren't you afraid of being raped?' he asked, so casually that it was a moment or two before Anna fully took it in.

'Oh! No, I . . . The thought never occurred to me!' She laughed, a hollow sound even to herself. Of course it had occurred to her. Often. But being tall and strong she had always reckoned she would be a match for any assailant. 'I'm big enough to take care of myself,' she pointed out.

'Suppose there were two of them. Or even a gang,' he said, coolly, and Anna shook her head, unwilling to discuss the matter any more.

'Look,' he went on, as she moved to go. 'I'm not off until ten but if you can hang around until then I'll drive you home. It won't take more than a couple of minutes,' he offered. Anna eyed him, doubtfully.

'Why on earth should you?' she asked, before she could stop herself, and his face darkened with temper.

'I mean . . . it's very kind of you,' she faltered, 'but I can't. I have to be home by ten,' she tried to explain. But he didn't understand.

'Surely another ten or fifteen minutes won't make any difference? Don't tell me father waits by the front door with a stop-watch!' he chuckled, and Anna fled, unable to take any more teasing.

It wasn't father but mother who sat, clock at the ready, watching and waiting for her only daughter's return. If she accepted Dr Alexandre's kind offer, Mother would be worried sick at the delay. And if Anna phoned home and explained that a doctor would be giving her a lift, that wouldn't suit her Mother either. She would be edgy and suspicious and ply Anna with questions about the doctor. Then she would lie sleepless, and the following morning her nurse would blame Anna for Mrs Curtis's bad night.

It was a vicious circle and the more Anna thought about it, the more her headache grew. If it hadn't been for Dr Alexandre she wouldn't have a headache, and it was one more black mark to chalk up against the senior medical registrar.

As it happened she was late leaving the ward and it was nearly a quarter to ten before she hurried to the main entrance, a borrowed umbrella at the ready. She paused before taking the plunge. Rain pelted down now, and the cold darkness was not inviting.

'Hey! Nurse Curtis!'

She whirled round, hoping she wasn't to be delayed still more. It would be after ten when she arrived home as it was.

Dr Alexandre, minus his white coat, hurried towards her. 'I managed to get off a bit early. I thought I'd missed you.' He sounded as if he had been running, his chest rising and falling unevenly, and Anna felt a stab of remorse for her earlier treatment of him.

He grinned suddenly, a lazy grin that touched his eyes as well as his lips, and Anna realised how attractive he was. Boyishly so, she thought, smiling back.

That direct gaze, those blue-grey eyes, were doing strange things to her heart, and she forced herself to think of Mike. He wouldn't be pleased if he could see her smiling into the registrar's eyes.

'I'll bring the car around. Save you getting wet, Nurse,' he offered. 'Sounds rather a mouthful—Nurse Curtis. It's Anna, isn't it?' he went on, still smiling, and she nodded, unable to speak.

'As we're off duty we'll be Anna and Rick, shall we? I won't be a minute.' Helping himself to the umbrella, he dashed out into the pouring rain, leaving a strangely exhilarated Anna to wait.

Rick! She was going to call him 'Rick'. Silently she tried the name out. Rick Alexandre. He was actually going to give her a lift and she wouldn't be late home after all. She would get him to stop the car a few yards from the door so that there wouldn't be an inquest. It was too good to be true!

'Anna! I've been here for hours!' Both the statement and the voice were so familiar to Anna that she didn't need to look. Just for a second she closed her eyes, wishing Mike Forster anywhere but at St Aidan's, waiting to give her a lift home in his car.

Mike's handsome face floated before her, and she almost believed it was an optical illusion. He wasn't there at all.

He grabbed her by the shoulders and shook her. 'Anna! For God's sake! I haven't got all night!' Because she still didn't move, he began to force her towards the entrance—just as a car tooted outside.

Anna, as if in a trance, saw Dr Alexandre get out of his car, a puzzled expression on his lean face. An expression which turned set and angry when Mike brushed his lips across Anna's.

Mike had his arm tucked firmly around Anna's waist as he pushed against the glass doors—and came face to face with Rick Alexandre.

CHAPTER THREE

MIKE and Dr Alexandre traded glances for a moment, then the registrar's contemptuous gaze met Anna's. A muscle worked at the corner of his mouth and his eyes blazed at her. They looked grey now, she thought dazedly. A stormy-grey, ready to pour down hail or sleet upon her head.

She licked her dry lips, then apologised meekly, while Mike looked on, his pale eyes going suspiciously from Anna to the doctor.

'I really am very sorry, Doctor, but my b . . . boyfriend came to give me a lift home,' she stammered, reddening under the doctor's silent scrutiny.

He shot a disapproving look at Mike, then shrugged. 'Glad you're getting a lift. Goodnight, Nurse.' He spun on his heel and strode back to his car.

Anna watched him drive away, no doubt back to the car-park, for he had a flat in the Nurses' Home. He had gone to a lot of trouble to offer her a lift and she felt ashamed.

'What's with him then? He a friend of yours?' Mike queried, and Anna shook her head.

'No, but it *was* kind of him to get the car out specially. We'll have to hurry, I must be in by ten, Mike!' she voiced her alarm, seeing that it was now nearly five to the hour.

'In by ten! A grown woman!' he jeered. 'Even Cinders was out till midnight!'

Anna bit her lip, understanding his annoyance. 'Mother worries a lot, Mike,' she protested. 'I told you she has heart trouble. She mustn't be upset.'

Still grumbling, Mike hurried her out to his car, a flashy red sports-car, and she eased herself into the only passenger seat, wishing there was more leg-room.

'Is it always going to be like this?' he demanded, sweeping out of the hospital entrance. 'Always hiding in corners, hurrying home because Mother mustn't be worried. Just when *are* you going to be free?'

He was angry and Anna couldn't blame him. 'I hope—as Mother improves—that I will be able to have more freedom. Once she realises that she isn't the invalid she believes she is things will be easier for me, for us,' she assured him, wondering herself how long it would be.

Mike clearly did not believe her and they drove home in silence. Lights blazed from all the down-stairs windows including her mother's bedroom, which was at the front of the old house.

When Mike moved to take her into his arms, Anna resisted, pushing against his broad chest. 'No, Mike. It's past ten now. Mother's nurse will be on the telephone to the hospital at any minute,' she said bitterly. Nurse Dixon was rather a burden sometimes, an over-fussy bulldozer type of woman with an over made-up, prematurely-lined face.

'Let them phone!' Mike snapped, brushing aside her hands and sweeping her masterfully into his arms. 'I want a goodnight kiss! It's the least you can do!' he pointed out. Then his lips were on hers and Anna closed her eyes blissfully.

This was love—it must be! With a happy sigh she snuggled even closer, and only half heard Mike's groan as his hands found her breasts. In her mind's eye she could see the outline of his dear lean face, feel those eyes boring into hers. Blue-grey eyes. Stormy eyes, filled with desire, and . . .

With a cry, she pulled herself free. Whilst enjoying Mike's embrace she had been thinking of Rick Alexandre!

'What's the matter?' Mike rasped, the frustration in his voice evident even to the dazed Anna.

He drew her into his arms again and she lay back limply, her mind far away. How could she be so wicked? She *loved* Mike. There ought to be no room in her thoughts or her heart for any other man.

Anger at her lack of response lent a cutting edge to Mike's voice and she didn't care for the expletives that came tripping off his tongue. 'There's a word for women like you!' he finished. 'They smile and laugh into a fellow's eyes. Tease him a little bit, let him kiss and fondle them. Yet when it comes to the nitty-gritty they just don't want to know!'

'Oh, Mike!' Anna wailed, feeling more wretched than ever. 'I didn't mean to tease, but I must go in! There isn't time for . . . for any more kisses.' Her voice trailed off, for she had suddenly realised she was *glad* there wasn't time. She needed to be alone, to think.

With a sigh Mike released her, and a dazed and troubled Anna hurried the remaining few yards to her home.

*

Wednesday dawned, cold but crisp, with a promise of sunshine later on. As Anna had suspected, her mother had complained a little when she knew Anna would be out all day. But when Anna promised to return home during her long afternoon break, all was well. Thankfully, neither Mother nor Mary Dixon queried why Anna had been late home on the Tuesday, accepting her hurried explanation that things were extra busy on the ward.

Throughout Tuesday night and during her walk to work the next day, Anna pondered on her interest in Dr Alexandre. That two penetrating blue-grey eyes could have such an effect on her was ridiculous. Yet she carried his image with her still as she strolled through the darkened hospital corridors on her way to Park Ward.

He had an interesting nose, she mused, smiling a little to herself, then turned, startled, as someone touched her shoulder.

It was Bryan Harris. 'Hello, green eyes! You were smiling to yourself; I distinctly saw your luscious lips curving!' he teased, and Anna hoped he couldn't see the faint colour that tinged her cheeks.

'Perhaps I have something to smile about. A whole day on women's medical is something to be savoured!' she laughed. Then seeing his puzzled frown, she explained that she was on a split duty.

'You aren't supposed to do split duties until the third year,' Bryan pointed out, his long face looking even more doleful than usual. 'None of us are, you know.'

'I know,' Anna agreed, 'but Sister wants her trained nurses on this afternoon because Dr Tester is coming back off sick leave to do a round. Every-

thing must be just so for him,' she added wryly, and
Bryan snorted.

'I've met him! Tall and dynamic, with chilly
brown eyes. Sister fancy him, does she?'

Anna turned surprised eyes on him. 'I'm not
sure. I think she's married, but . . .' She hesitated.
She had been about to say she thought Sister
Noakes might fancy Dr Alexandre but she didn't
want to repeat gossip—didn't want to believe it
herself, either.

Yet it was possible. They were not far apart in
age, she guessed. Dr Alexandre was in his early
thirties, she judged, if that. He was obviously keen
to get to the top. Sister Noakes could do worse than
hitch her star to his. This Dr Tester sounded attractive, though. For some reason Anna fervently
hoped that Sister *did* fancy the consultant rather
than the senior registrar. The morning passed swiftly for Anna. Now that she was getting used to the
ward routine she didn't find the work so hard.
During the morning she saw the house doctor, Dr
Wilmott, in the ward, together with Dr Alexandre,
and hurriedly bent her head to her task of tidying
Mr Cumming's locker. She didn't want to see Dr
Alexandre—Rick. There was nothing she could say
to him, other than to apologise, once again.

Anyway, she told herself crossly, he ought to be
pleased she'd saved him a journey. He lived in so
could hardly say he would have dropped her off on
his way home. Where was his home, anyway? she
pondered, trying to imagine him in a setting like her
own. She had never been to the Channel Islands so
had difficulty in visualising them.

She presumed Dr Alexandre didn't have a wife

but did he have a girlfriend? Perhaps one in Jersey?

'Nurse!' At last Mr Cumming's voice penetrated Anna's private world, and she jumped up, smiling at the patient. Remembering he was blind, she put the smile into her voice instead, seeing from the corner of her eye that the two doctors were approaching with Pauline Wilson.

She turned her attention to her patient, hoping Dr Alexandre wouldn't stop at that particular bed. 'I've tidied your locker, Mr Cumming. On the top now is just your jug of fruit juice and a glass. Do get someone to reach it for you, though,' she warned, and the man nodded.

'Did I hear Dr Alexandre?' he asked loudly, and Anna squirmed, watching the registrar change direction.

'Good morning, Mr Cumming. A lovely morning with even a touch of bird-song, I believe!' Dr Alexandre laughed, and Anna lowered her eyes submissively, waiting for the registrar to move on.

'Never! Is there really, doc? Not in December. It isn't the courting season yet!' Mr Cumming chortled.

'It must be my hearing then,' Dr Alexandre agreed, not appearing to notice Anna, though she was really too tall to miss.

She swallowed nervously, knowing she ought to say something yet not knowing what.

'You must be in love, Doctor! That's what it is,' Mr Cumming assured him, and Anna's heart gave a funny little lurch and dropped several inches. She held her breath, waiting for the registrar to reply.

'Could be, Mr Cumming,' Rick Alexandre agreed, then moved away, still without acknowledging Anna, who silently carried away the rubbish Mr Cumming had asked her to dispose of.

He could be in love. But with whom? Sister Noakes? No. Anna shook her head, once in the safety of the linen-cupboard, which was also on her list for tidying. Indeed she had done little else that morning and wondered if her presence was strictly necessary.

'Anna.' Pauline Wilson followed her to the linen-cupboard a few minutes later. 'Sister says as you aren't busy she's going to lend you to Coppice, next door. They want a patient taken to X-ray and can't spare a nurse. Will you go now, please? Then you can take an early lunch and go off till four-thirty, Sister says.' The third-year vanished, and Anna gave an exasperated sigh.

Now she was to run general errands! Still, it was better than staying there, feeling Dr Alexandre's contempt. Four-thirty was early to return to duty, she mused, knowing it ought to be five o'clock, but Sister *was* allowing her to go to lunch early.

By the time Anna had wheeled her patient to X-ray and seen the queue she knew her lunch wasn't going to be an early one. Bryan and Sheila were there, from her set, and she edged her patient nearer to them.

The patient, Mrs Norton, was over eighty but sprightly enough, according to the Coppice Ward Staff Nurse. Her wrist had been troubling her so much in hospital that an X-ray had been ordered. The patient chatted non-stop about her stay at St Aidan's while they waited for the X-ray.

Anna listened attentively, even though the old

lady tended to repeat herself. Consequently, she had little opportunity to talk to her colleagues, but she heard Bryan tell Sheila Haggerty about the split duty, and Sheila, a sharp-eyed troublemaker, raised her brows in disbelief.

'You're on again at five then?' she called across to Anna, who shook her head, her mind half on what Mrs Norton was telling her about her great-grandson.

'Half-past four,' Anna said, absently. If she had been alert, she would have noticed the pleased way Sheila sat back, lips pursed determinedly. Anna knew well that Sheila liked to complain about the hospital or the training if she could.

This was Sheila's second hospital. She had started her training at a London teaching hospital but found the discipline too restrictive. At least that was the reason she gave everyone. Anna had her doubts and believed Sheila and the hospital had parted by mutual consent!

It was nearly one o'clock by the time Anna returned Mrs Norton to the ward. Then she had to listen to the old lady's reminiscences once again, as Mrs Norton insisted that Anna should help settle her in a chair by the bed for her lunch. Eventually Anna was free, and dragging on her raincoat as she ran, she hared downstairs towards the entrance. Lunch would be ruined and Mother would be in hysterics. Anna could, from vast experience, picture the scene all too clearly.

She ran outside, glad to see the pale winter sun, then nearly collided with a man on her short cut across the car-park.

Strong arms steadied her when she would have

fallen, and a deep, masculine voice asked if she was all right.

Flushed and breathless, Anna gazed up—into a handsome if heavy-featured face, and dark eyes. 'Oh! I'm very sorry!' she said, struggling to regain her breath. Was this a consultant? she wondered in dismay. Probably he was just admin, but he was very well-dressed.

'The devil himself chasing you, is he?' the deep, amused voice asked, brown eyes assessing her shrewdly.

'No! I'm sorry, really. I'm late for lunch. That's all.' Anna longed to resume her wild run but the dark man's hand was still holding her wrist, where her pulse was pumping away.

'Is lunch far away?' he asked, releasing her.

'Only Brightling Hill. If you will excuse me?' Without waiting for his permission, she scurried away. She wondered again, briefly, who the man was, but her thoughts were mainly for her mother, who was sure to be worried and distressed.

Mother *was* worried and distressed. Though distraught might have been a better word, Anna thought glumly, eyeing mother's pale, tear-stained face and shaking hands.

Jennifer Curtis had been an actress before she married and everything was over-dramatised. Even before her coronary every little setback was magnified a million times. Anna suspected her mother enjoyed acting, loved a meaty, tearful scene, but she would never voice her suspicions. Actresses and actors lived in a permanent world of make-believe, Anna reckoned, and who was she to insist they lived in this dreary world? Let Mother enjoy her scenes, insist on star-billing. If she was happy, then so was Anna.

The fact that Anna had no social life and few friends didn't matter just then, as she hugged her mother, smoothing back the still fine red-brown hair. Hair that was greying rapidly now, adding to her mother's grief.

'I got held up, Mother. I had to take an old lady to X-ray, then on the way out of the hospital I nearly knocked a man down!' Anna laughed, trying to cheer her mother up.

'Oh?' Jennifer's tears dried miraculously, as she signalled to Mrs Jenkins to bring in the lunch. 'What sort of man? A handsome consultant?'

'Well, he might have been,' Anna acknowledged slowly. 'Anyway he was well-built so I didn't knock him flying!'

Anna hurried upstairs to change, the brown-eyed stranger vanishing from her thoughts.

When a refreshed and well-fed Anna returned to the ward, she was immediately summoned to Sister's office, where Sister Noakes eyed her crossly. Anna's heart lurched as she met the cool gaze of Rick Alexandre, who was perched on a corner of Sister's desk, long legs swinging idly. He, too, appeared cross.

'Nurse Curtis,' Sister began, sharply, 'if you had some objection to working a split today why didn't you come to see me?'

Anna opened her mouth, but Sister waved her to silence. 'I have,' she continued, her scarlet mouth set, 'been taken to task by Mrs Lucas. She told me that no matter how short we are, first and second-years are not to do split duties. Except in emergen-

cy, of course. Unless . . .' She paused, and gazed
reprovingly at Anna, who by now was beginning to
see the light. Someone had obviously complained
to Mrs Lucas, the Principal Nursing Officer
(Education), and it didn't take much thought to
work out who was the culprit.

'Unless,' Sister went on, 'the student agrees and
provided it is only an occasional split duty. I was
under the impression that you *did* agree, Nurse.'

'I did, Sister. Really. I could understand that you
wanted your trained staff for Dr Tester's round, so
I didn't mind,' Anna assured her. Sister raised her
heavily-pencilled brows.

'Why, then, did you go behind my back and
complain?'

'I did not, Sister. I . . . I happened to mention my
split duty to someone else in my set and word of it
must have got back to one of the tutors,' Anna
explained hesitantly, not wanting to get Sheila or
Bryan into trouble but not wanting to be in Sister's
bad books, either.

'I see,' Sister said, doubtfully. Then she glanced
at Dr Alexandre, who shrugged.

'The grapevine works quickly here. Or so I've
found,' he said wryly. 'Even crediting me with a
fiancée I haven't got!'

Sister laughed, good-humour restored, then told
Anna she could go. Surprised and rather cross,
Anna left, still wondering if Sister believed her. She
was pleased to hear that the registrar wasn't engaged, anyway!

The evening hours were not long enough for
everything that had to be done, Anna found. Ruth
Barratt was on, she was glad to see, feeling that she

had found a friend in the cheery nursing auxiliary.

'Mr Pearson has been moaning again, Anna,' Ruth said, chuckling. 'He's lost his lower set now, he claims. Says one of the nurses must have mislaid it.'

'That isn't true! He hides his dentures under the pillow, then complains when we put them in his locker!' Anna protested. 'I don't know why he doesn't wear them.'

'They don't fit, that's why. My father doesn't wear his dentures very often,' Ruth confided, keeping step with Anna as they walked down the ward. 'If people don't wear them for a long while then suddenly decide they will, often the dentures don't fit any more. The face changes shape without teeth to support it, as you know. Eventually the dentures seem too big and people go to their dentists, complaining that their false teeth don't fit their mouth any more!'

'It's their own fault for not wearing them regularly,' Anna agreed, wondering how she would cope if ever she had artificial teeth. It was something she didn't care to think about just yet!

Mr Pearson, of course, blamed Anna for losing his lower dentures. Although a miserable, unhappy man at the best of times, he seemed to take a special delight in annoying Anna, and took every opportunity he could to complain about her. As this was only her third day on the ward, she wondered ruefully what she'd done to deserve such treatment.

'You big 'uns are all alike,' Mr Pearson grumbled, as Anna patiently turned out his locker for him, but without success.

'I can't help being tall,' she pointed out, kindly. 'I'm sorry but your teeth aren't here. You didn't give them to your wife to take home?' she asked, hopefully, and was dismayed to see an angry red flush spread across the patient's cheeks.

'She ain't my wife and it's none of your business, you thieving monkey!' he cried, loudly enough to be heard in the office.

'Mr Pearson!' Anna said, severely. 'I don't *need* your dentures! There's nothing wrong with my own teeth. See.' She opened her mouth, displaying neat, even white teeth, and Mr Pearson had the grace to look ashamed.

'Well, they ain't here,' he muttered, picking up his newspaper and ignoring Anna's further efforts at conversation.

Who, she wondered, making her way to the day-room, *was* the big-boned woman who visited Mr Pearson so regularly? Visiting hours were very relaxed at St Aidan's, as the hospital authorities believed it was in the patients' best interests to have visitors at various times during the day rather than having them all sandwiched between seven and eight in the evening.

Despite her short time on the ward, Anna had seen Mr Pearson's visitor several times already so the woman obviously cared. She frowned, wondering if the big woman was his daughter. She just might be, but somehow Anna doubted it. Whoever she was, she deserved great credit for looking after such a miserable man!

Anna was soon engrossed in a game of ludo with two of the older men. The day-room was warm and comfortable, with plenty of old but still elegant armchairs and a settee, all donated by the local League of Friends.

One or two members of the League were coming in during the evening, and she'd been warned to keep an eye open for them. There were only two visitors in the day-room, both seemingly relatives so Anna relaxed a little.

When she won a hard round of ludo she beamed at everybody, pleased at her small success—the first that evening, and old Mr Mitchell chuckled.

'You would think you'd won an Oscar, you look that pleased!' he chortled, and Anna laughed.

'I'm sorry but I'm not generally a lucky person. At snakes and ladders I find all the biggest snakes! My mother always wins. It's a standing joke by now,' she added, then a shadow fell across the ludo board and she glanced up, the smile still hovering about her lips, green eyes sparkling.

Dr Alexandre's eyes gazed steadily into hers, and her laughter faded away as she politely began to rise. Because there wasn't much room around the small table she had difficulty in getting up, then the registrar put his hand on her shoulder and pressed her down again.

'Sit still, Anna. I'll join you,' he announced, while Anna sat, frozen into her seat now. Rick was going to play ludo with them! Senior registrars had no time for that sort of thing. Why, the poor man must be asleep on his feet!

Anna's soft heart went out to him and her sympathy must have communicated itself to the registrar in some way, for he smiled into her eyes. 'I'm not dead yet, Anna. I've got enough strength left to trounce all three of you at ludo!'

Nervously, Anna made room for him. Because there was so little space he sat very close to her. Disturbingly close, long legs brushing against hers. She tensed, wishing he would sit further away. How could she concentrate on the game with this attractive man so near?

Yet you love Mike! a little voice reminded her, and she sighed, causing the registrar to pause as he was about to rattle the dice.

'Cold, Anna?' he asked softly, and she shook her head and managed to laugh.

'No, I was just thinking, you are probably the ludo champion of Jersey and I won't win any more!'

He raised a dark brow, his expression quizzical. 'How did you know I came from Jersey?'

Mr Mitchell saved Anna from answering just then. 'One of us asked about the unusual spelling of your name, Doctor. Staff Nurse said as how you were from the Channel Islands,' he put in, and the registrar seemed to relax.

'A regular Jersey potato, I am!' he laughed, and Anna watched, fascinated, at the way his eyes crinkled with laughter. His face was full of laughter lines she noted, before dropping her gaze to her coloured counter. It was a face made for mirth and she wondered why she hadn't noticed before.

True, he wasn't classically handsome in the way that Mike Forster was. His nose was too long, his brows too heavy . . .

'You have just moved Mr Mitchell's counter, Nurse!' a laughing voice broke into her thoughts, and Anna flinched as if struck. She gazed at the counters. Dr Alexandre was right. Hers was red.

Had she really moved the green one? She bit her lip, embarrassed.

'Colour-blind, are you, Nurse?' Mr Taylor asked, and all three men laughed.

'Must be in love,' Mr Mitchell announced, causing the registrar to eye her thoughtfully.

'Are you, Anna?' he asked, peering at her averted face so that she was forced to meet his gaze at last.

Those steady eyes were stormy-grey again and Anna ran her tongue nervously over her dry lips before shaking her head. 'No. Not exactly,' she parried, then turned to Mr Mitchell.

'It's your turn with the dice, Mr Mitchell,' she said, gaily, but even to her own ears her voice sounded on the verge of breaking. Dr Alexandre had no right to ask such a question!

The game was nearly finished, with Dr Alexandre heading for the winning post, when the League of Friends committee members arrived. The registrar, who sat facing the door, saw them first, and Anna's eyes followed his gaze.

Two women hovered in the doorway, with Staff Nurse Powell fussing around them. Then the younger woman, a tall brunette, beamed at their group, and Anna's eyes went from one patient to the other as she rose. But the smile was for Dr Alexandre, she saw now, as he went forward, hand outstretched, face wreathed in smiles.

'Ricky! I'd no idea you worked here!' the brunette trilled, taking his hand and holding on to it with both of hers.

Anna watched, fascinated, as the brunette and the registrar stood, smiling, apparently oblivious to those around them. She turned away, her eyes suspiciously bright.

They continued their interrupted game, Anna moving the orange counter which had been the registrar's. But her eyes and ears were busy, as she tried to hear the registrar's conversation. The older woman and the Staff Nurse walked among the patients, exchanging a few words with them, but Dr Alexandre and his lady friend stood in the farthest corner, their voices low, and Anna, for some reason, wanted to hurl the ludo-board out of the day-room window.

'Raining again, Nurse,' Mr Mitchell commented, as the game finished, with Dr Alexandre's orange counter the winner.

Anna shivered. 'That's all I need. A walk home in the dark and cold!' she said lightly, unaware that the registrar and his companion had drifted back within earshot.

'If you aren't getting a lift tonight, Nurse, I'll drop you off,' Dr Alexandre said evenly, and Anna turned questioning eyes on him.

'I have to go out so you may as well have a lift,' he went on, his voice cold, and Anna stammered her thanks.

She smiled tentatively at the woman by his side, and the smile was returned, but guardedly. Dr Alexandre performed the introductions and Anna was treated to a full inspection, the brunette's dark eyes missing no detail. She was Mrs Margaret Warwick of the League of Friends, and the registrar gave Anna a run-down of the good works the League performed, the donations they made, the cheer they brought to the patients, and this time

Mrs Warwick gave Anna a genuinely friendly smile, obviously pleased at the registrar's praise.

Anna did her best to look impressed, though her one impulse was to escape from the registrar and his friend. Mrs Warwick seemed older than Rick, Anna put her age at around forty. Probably she wasn't a friend in the way Anna had at first thought. She supposed Mrs Warwick was the wife of someone important and had to be deferred to.

Dr Alexandre promised to be at the front entrance promptly at nine-thirty and told Staff Nurse Powell that Anna must leave on time.

When nine-thirty came, she couldn't control her excitement. It was stupid of her. The man was only offering her a lift home! But Mike had been the only man in her life. So being taken home by another man was something of a novelty to her, and she hummed a tune as she hurried to the main door—to see the smiling face of Mrs Warwick who also, seemingly, was awaiting a lift from Dr Alexandre.

CHAPTER FOUR

ANNA's bubble of happiness burst and the smile she gave Margaret Warwick was strained.

'The rain is quite heavy now,' Mrs Warwick commented, and Anna obediently gazed through the glass doors, seeing nothing, and hearing nothing save the pounding of her own heart.

Naturally he had a reason for going out, a reason for leaving early. He was taking Mrs Warwick somewhere. Out to dinner perhaps?

Anna was surprised that the woman was still there but she must have considered Dr Alexandre worth waiting for. And he was, Anna acknowledged, green eyes pensive. She had so wanted to sit beside him in a companionable silence. Now her evening was spoilt. She would be relegated to the back seat, forced to watch Mrs Warwick smile into those blue-grey eyes, see their arms touch as the woman leaned towards him . . .

There was something cold and hard in her stomach and it wasn't the canteen supper. She barely recognised it as jealousy. It couldn't be. Could it? She loved Mike Forster. One day, when Mother was better, they could bring their tepid romance out into the open. Become lovers, even. Something stirred within her as she waited patiently for the registrar. She wanted marriage. There was nothing as good as marriage, no matter what Mike said. But . . .

'Ah, he's here!' Mrs Warwick's delighted voice broke into Anna's troubled thoughts, and she smiled politely.

The glass doors parted and she raised her head, a bright smile fixed to her face. He mustn't know that she minded. Dark brown eyes and a dark brown voice to match appeared before her, and she gasped. They belonged to the man she'd bumped into earlier.

Mrs Warwick put her hand on the man's arm as he pushed the door open for her. Their mingled laughter drifted back to Anna who stood, bemused, hardly aware that another man had entered as the others left.

Dr Alexandre touched her shoulder lightly, as she stood staring after the couple. His eyes followed hers and he must have misread her expression, for he said, bitterly,

'After consultants now, are you? Sorry I'm only a humble registrar! Dr Tester's way out of your league, Anna.'

She opened her mouth to explain but wasn't given the chance as he almost pushed her out into the cold, rainy night. His car, from what she could see of it in the light from the hospital, looked new. It was certainly roomy and Anna sighed with relief.

Without a word, Dr Alexandre settled himself beside her and set the car in motion. She stole a quick glance at his face, which was set and angry, and decided not to risk any conversation. She might get her head bitten off. Besides, it was his mistake. If that was Dr Tester and he chose to believe she fancied him, let him. She couldn't care less *what* he thought.

They were nearly at Brightling Hill before Anna broke the strained silence. 'Please don't trouble to take me right up to the house, Doctor. I can walk the last few yards.'

He grunted, and Anna's temper rose. 'Waiting for you in the shrubbery, is he?' he asked, suddenly.

'Who?'

'That young lad. The one with blackheads and crinkly hair. He'll be wet by now. Shouldn't think he's still there. I'll take you to your door, if you tell me which one,' he offered, his voice infuriatingly calm.

'For one thing, Mike has *not* got blackheads! And for another, I don't *want* to be taken to my door!' she said, sharply. 'It . . . it worries my mother. She's been very ill.'

'I'm sorry. Though I should think she would prefer you to be given a lift home. Doesn't she worry that you nip home across the rec?'

'She doesn't know,' Anna admitted. 'She doesn't really think about it. I'll have to take driving lessons and get a car.'

'Which house is it, then?'

She saw they were parked outside her own house, where a light burned outside the front door. 'You're right here. This is Millstones.'

'What a name!' he chuckled, ill-humour gone. 'And is it a millstone?'

'Well . . . yes, I suppose it is. The house is far too big for us, really, but Mother has a full-time nurse. She lives in and so does the housekeeper,' Anna explained.

His steady gaze held hers and Anna's voice

trailed off. He'll think I'm boasting was her last coherent thought, as his lips met hers in a tantalisingly brief kiss.

'Goodnight, Anna. Sleep well.' He sounded amused, and Anna's lips tightened ominously. He was making fun of her! Probably he could see she was inexperienced. He thought her a naïve little nobody and was anxious to show his prowess with women.

'Goodnight, Dr Alexandre,' she said primly, then spoiled her exit by having difficulty finding the door catch in the dark.

'It's right there, Anna. Look, you pull it up, not down,' the registrar said patiently, and Anna flinched as he reached across her body to open the door. She heard a faint sound as though he was trying not to laugh, and she longed to disappear, so acute was her embarrassment.

'Th . . . thank you, Doctor,' she managed, glad to escape from his nearness.

'Don't forget it will soon be Christmas, Anna. You'll be on Park Ward, won't you?'

Surprised, Anna said she would, wondering why he should care. 'Good. We'll have a lovely time. I'll bring plenty of mistletoe. You won't be able to escape then! Bye!'

Red-faced, Anna hurried up to the porch—to find Mary Dixon hovering by the front door, her pekinese nose positively twitching with curiosity.

'Good evening, Mary,' Anna said, distantly, 'it was kind of you to watch out for me,' she added, hanging up her raincoat, then making for the stairs before the woman could speak.

In the safety of her room, Anna collapsed on to

the bed, breathing heavily. The nerve of that man! Bringing mistletoe just to annoy her. He would enjoy her embarrassment as he forced his kisses on her in full view of the patients!

'You've met your match, Rick Alexandre!' she said, aloud. 'No way am *I* providing free entertainment.'

Of course Nurse Dixon had told Anna's mother that she'd had a lift home, and her mother's eyes were wary as Anna hurried into see her. She was in bed, a big tester bed, surrounded by books and magazines, and a copy of *The Stage*. The house was centrally-heated so she was warm enough in her cream lacy bed-jacket and silk nightgown. Anna was struck afresh by her mother's beauty. Only the greying hair suggested middle age was approaching, yet even so, Jennifer Curtis did not look forty-nine.

It seemed a shame that because of her heart attack she'd given up life, or very nearly. Now she considered herself an invalid and insisted that the household revolve around her, and that her only child should be obedient and not seek a life outside the home, Anna thought, rebelliously. It was so unfair!

'Mary says you got a lift home, dear. Was it someone nice?' Jennifer asked casually enough, but Anna wasn't deceived.

'No one important, Mother,' she parried. 'But I've been meaning to speak to you—about having to come home in the dark and rain, I mean. Couldn't I have a car and driving lessons?'

Anna waited for the world to come crashing about her ears, but nothing happened and faint hope glowed in her eyes. Her mother appeared to be seriously considering the idea, but finally she shook her head.

'I don't think so, Anna. I should be *so* worried. There are so many careless drivers about these days and you never know. Then there is the expense,' she sighed, putting one delicate, fine-boned hand over her heart in a gesture Anna knew so well.

'I would be a careful driver, Mother,' Anna said, stubborn for once. 'And don't worry about the cost. Daddy left me quite a bit, you know, and I've hardly spent any. I've enough for a Mini, I think.'

There was a shocked silence, then Jennifer gave a strangled gasp and lay back against the lace-trimmed pillows. 'It's too, too bad of you!' she gasped, red spots of colour on her cheeks. 'You know I mustn't be upset! Where *is* Mary?' She rang for her nurse before Anna could stop her.

Now Anna had the bit between her teeth she wasn't going to pull up. Her mother wasn't *that* ill, her GP had said so himself.

'Do you know I take a short-cut through the recreation ground, Mother?' she asked quietly, just as Mary Dixon came bustling in. 'I could be raped, you know. Or mugged and left lying in a pool of blood,' Anna went on, relentlessly.

Jennifer sat bolt upright, eyes wide with astonishment, her heart pain forgotten. 'I'd no idea! Isn't there another way home?'

'Only a roundabout route. It takes nearly twice as long and that isn't terribly well-lit either,' Anna told her. She heard Nurse Dixon snort.

'It may not be for me to say, but you've no right

upsetting your mother like that!' Mary Dixon said sharply.

Anna was about to retort but aid came from an unexpected quarter. Jennifer said, quietly, 'The girl is right, Mary. She ought not to have that long walk. And in the dark, too!' Jennifer shuddered delicately, then opened her arms to Anna.

'I *do* understand, my darling,' Jennifer said. 'And you *shall* have a car. In the meantime you must have a taxi home when you're on late turn.'

'I would have done but I didn't want to worry you. Anyway, there isn't much of a taxi service around here,' Anna said ruefully. 'Only old Mr Partridge and his two sons.'

'Still, if you booked in advance, had a standing order, so to speak, you should be all right.'

Anna smiled down at her mother. To hear her plan Anna's taxi-journeys anyone would think it was a major operation! Still, it was good that she was taking an interest in Anna's welfare, it augered well for the future.

Faced with mother and daughter in agreement for once, Mary Dixon dared not say more, and Anna would not have been human if she hadn't been glad to see the starchy little SEN taken down a peg or two. Nurse Dixon had taken delight in thwarting Anna at every turn since she'd started her training. And that was the crux of the matter, Anna thought, Mary was afraid that Anna would shortly know more than her and would try to give her orders.

But that wasn't Anna's way. If she had to give orders then she would, but an experienced SEN was worth more than a very green first-year student nurse, and Anna was glad of Mary's expertise with heart cases when it came to looking after her mother.

Thursday was another busy day on the ward but Anna didn't mind. She had Friday and Saturday as her rest days. True, the two days promised to be long and empty, but there were Christmas cards to be written and some sewing she ought to do.

She sighed as she prepared to do the umpteenth TPR round. Cards and sewing. What an empty life hers was. Wouldn't it be lovely to share her days off with a young man? If only she and Mike could be free.

She considered the matter, her expression serious, unaware that she was being observed. Tomorrow she and this special someone might go for a long walk if the threatened snow didn't come. Or even if it *did* snow—they could throw snowballs at each other, Anna thought, delighted with the idea. A dreamy smile curved her pretty mouth. Then, after a late lunch, they would prepare to go out for the evening.

First dinner at some romantic spot in Southampton. Trout, steak, then an impossibly fattening meringue topped with fresh cream and chocolate sauce! Afterwards, they would take in a show or perhaps go on to a night-club.

Anna had never been to a night-club and thought she might not like the smoky, overheated atmosphere, but it would make a change . . .

Her smile faded and she gazed sadly at her fob-watch. Time for temperatures, pulses and respirations. She wasn't paid to daydream.

'Happy, Nurse Curtis?' a voice asked, and Dr Alexandre strolled into the ward, immaculate in his white coat, the lines of good-humour on his face deepening as Anna blushed.

'Oh! Yes, I'm happy,' she assured him, wondering if she had spoken any of her daydreams aloud. 'Sister is in her office,' she ventured.

'Is she? That's nice for her, isn't it?' he said agreeably, eyes twinkling at Anna.

Despite her determination not to weaken, a reluctant smile came to Anna's face.

'Your eyes light up like candles—Christmas candles,' Dr Alexandre said softly. She wasn't aware of him moving but suddenly he was within touching distance and how she longed to touch him.

She wanted to put her hands on his face, smooth away the laughter lines, gaze deeply into those steady eyes . . . She pulled herself together, aware that her expression might be giving her away. 'Excuse me, please. I have to take the men's temperatures.'

He moved aside to let her pass, and disappointment stabbed her.

'I'll bet their temperatures are always higher when you're around!' he chuckled to her retreating back, but Anna pretended not to hear. The cheek of the man!

They had another new patient now, a diabetic. John Snelling was a year or two younger than Anna and had been admitted for stabilisation of his regime of diet and insulin. He confidently expected to be out within a week but Anna knew better. Staff Nurse had told her he would be kept in over Christmas, if they could spare the bed, because

John over-indulged himself and he could die at Christmas if there was no one to watch his diet.

Although intelligent, he seemed incapable of denying himself anything—and this applied to girls as well as food. He'd already boasted that he had a girlfriend for each day of the week.

His face lit up as Anna approached. Patients' thermometers were kept in a phial at the head of their beds, just under the notice giving their name and religion, and Anna moved forward to take John's thermometer, her mind still on the registrar. He had a lovely smile. Not as nice as Mike's, of course. Or was it?

'Ow!' John Snelling's long, thin arm wrapped itself around Anna's leg, his fingers caressing her thigh.

'Let me go!' she whispered furiously, anxious not to disturb the others.

John grinned up at her, his freckled face alight with laughter, and she hadn't the heart to be too cross with him. He *was* rather sweet. Even so, he had to be kept in his place or it would be another black mark for Nurse Curtis!

Unfortunately, Mr Pearson saw the intimate gesture and began bellowing for Staff Nurse.

Scared of being taken to task yet again, Anna cried, 'Please, Mr Pearson! I'll be with you in a moment!'

'You won't!' the old man snapped, just as Sister Noakes glided into view. 'You're too busy letting that dirty so and so do what he likes to worry about we old ones!'

'What *is* the matter?' Sister Noakes's voice was icy as she spoke to Mr Pearson and her brown eyes were cold as they rested on Anna, who fidgeted uncomfortably. 'You know the patients must be kept quiet, Nurse Curtus,' Sister went on.

'Yes, Sister. I'm sorry but I was just going to take Mr Snelling's temperature when Mr Pearson started shouting,' Anna explained, hoping that neither of the men would mention John Snelling's wandering hands.

But she hoped in vain. 'It were that dirty little blighter, Sister!' Mr Pearson pointed an accusing finger at John. 'He were putting his hand up Nurse's skirt!'

Anna blushed, John Snelling almost choked with laughter, and there were smirks and muffled laughter from the other men. Anna waited, terrified, for Sister to fly into a rage.

Instead, Sister Noakes permitted herself a tight smile. 'When male patients start touching up the nurses, it's a sign they are getting better!'

Astonished, Anna watched Sister's starchy figure disappear in the direction of the office, and John smirked. 'See, she likes me. I knew she did!'

'So it would seem!' Anna said, heart still thudding at thought of what might have been. Mr Pearson sat back against his pillows looking cross, and she hurriedly did the rest of the TRPs, leaving Mr Pearson and John Snelling to last to give their temperatures time to cool down.

As she finished writing up Mr Pearson's chart, she saw Sister and Dr Alexandre walking purposefully towards her, and she trembled. Dr Alexandre was cross, his face set. Even his walk, the way he held himself, seemed angry. What, she wondered, had she done now?

But they stopped at John Snelling's bed and Sister began to give the boy a gentle yet firm telling-off. The registrar left her and came towards Anna as she hurriedly replaced Mr Pearson's chart.

'Can't you do *anything* right?' he asked, as soon as they were out of earshot of the patients. 'Do you *have* to stir people up all the time? *Must* you be the centre of attention?' he went on relentlessly, his firm jaw jutting pugnaciously. Anna's eyes flashed with anger.

'I'm very sorry, sir,' she said quietly. She would have liked to tell him a few home truths but knew no one would take her side. If she cheeked a senior registrar she would be reported to Mrs Lucas and possibly removed from the ward.

Head held high, she marched back to the ward, feeling Dr Alexandre's eyes boring into her. Once inside, she pulled the door to and collapsed, trembling, on to the only chair. Tears pricked her eyelids and she couldn't stop the shaking. Only her heart felt numb. Whatever she did, it was wrong in his eyes. She believed now that the registrar had heard Mr Pearson accuse John and had told Sister she must deal with the matter more severely then she had done. Sister thought it no more than a sign that John was getting better, his condition stabilising, but Dr Alexandre thought otherwise.

He was a prude, Anna decided. When he was a medical student *he* must have caressed a few girls. The miserable creature! Perhaps he didn't like her because she was tall and red-haired, she thought illogically. Try as she might, she could find no logical reason for his attitude towards her.

Sister called Anna into the office just before

four-thirty and told her firmly that she must stop antagonising Dr Alexandre.

'But Sister, I don't!' Anna cried. 'At least not knowingly. Whatever I do he finds fault with. Perhaps he doesn't like tall women,' she went on, reflectively.

Sister raised an eyebrow. 'He doesn't keep finding fault with *me*,' she pointed out, 'and I'm only a couple of inches shorter than you.'

Anna considered their height difference more like four or five inches than a couple, but refrained from saying so. 'Maybe he doesn't like first-year students.'

Sister shrugged. 'Few senior registrars even *notice* first-years, so I shouldn't think it's that. Anyway, keep a low profile whenever he's around. He seems a good-humoured man, but there's no point in living dangerously, Nurse.'

Anna didn't think him at all good-humoured, but didn't argue with Sister Noakes. Although, she mused, as she made her way home a few minutes later, he *was* good-humoured at times. He enjoyed a laugh with the patients and with Sister Noakes. It was something about her he didn't like. Some personality trait of Anna's that caused his hackles to rise.

Feeling alone and friendless, Anna began her wintry walk through the recreation ground. Even Mike wouldn't be around to cheer her up. Tomorrow he was working and at the weekend he was going home to Liverpool to see his parents. He often went home at weekends. He was a good son to them, Anna thought warmly. And she loved him for his many kind little ways.

That she loved him because he was the only young man she'd allowed to get close to her emotionally, Anna didn't stop to think. She was sure that it was a deep, abiding love that would last until death. She could see Mike's faults and was prepared to make allowances for them. He was hopelessly untidy. He spilled cigarette ash over everything. And he was a heavy smoker. That might not be classed as a fault, she acknowledged, but it was worrying. She'd attended health education lectures at school and had learned the dangers of smoking to excess. He might cut it down, just to please her, though. He had promised to do so before, but his promises were never kept, she reflected. That was another fault. He could not be trusted to keep his word.

Anna walked on, angry with herself for dwelling on the disadvantages of loving Mike Forster. The good outweighed the bad. Anyway, was *she* so free from faults that she could sit in judgment on another human being?

She paused, taking stock of her surroundings. All of a sudden she felt uneasy, as though millions of eyes were watching her. It was almost dusk now and although she turned and looked this way and that, she saw no one, heard nothing—until Mike's voice drifted over to her from out of the blue, 'Late again, Anna,' he said, bitterly.

She gasped, then ran into his open arms. 'Mike! Where were you? Were you following me? I . . . I was so frightened!' she said, clinging to him in her relief.

'Anna! You big baby!' he laughed, his hands gently soothing her.

She snuggled closer. Her hospital raincoat was no great protection against the chill of the late afternoon, and she felt Mike's warmth spreading through to her. When he began to kiss her as they strolled, she accepted his kisses passively, her numb face only gradually responding.

'Hey! Come on, Anna!' he grated.

'It's cold!' she protested, lifting her face for another kiss. This time the answering pressure of her lips left him in no doubt that she was enjoying his love-making, and his arms tightened.

'Mm! You're thawing out nicely!' Mike joked, stopping near the lamppost at the foot of Brightling Hill. 'I used to think you were a real old maid! Comes of having mummy watching over you all the time, I guess,' he went on, half to himself. Anna wriggled out of his arms.

'That isn't fair, Mike! I . . . I'm not used to free love! All this jumping into bed with whoever asks you. It isn't my way. I'm sorry if I seem prudish,' she went on, but Mike's mouth came down on hers as he drew her roughly towards him, and she had no breath left to argue.

With a groan he pushed her away, and she staggered for a second, eyes wide with astonishment.

'Listen Anna, this is no good! All this.' Mike waved his large hands about to encompass the setting, the winter's day, the very fact that they had to meet secretly.

'I know. I *do* understand, Mike' she emphasised, 'but with Mother as she is . . .'

'I'll bet if I were a doctor or some fancy surgeon she'd be nice enough to me!' he said sulkily, and Anna lowered her eyes.

He could be right. Dr Alexandre or Dr Tester might be welcome. So long as they did not evince a strong interest in Anna. Mother wouldn't want to lose her only daughter, not even in marriage to a doctor.

'Perhaps if she thought we were serious, Mike, she would come to accept you,' Anna said slowly. 'She wants me to be happy.'

'Does she?' he asked bitterly, his wide mouth sullen and ugly in the unkind light. 'I don't think your mother cares for anyone but herself!' He paused to light a cigarette and took a long drag on it before he went on, 'I'm leaving soon, Anna. Got a chance of promotion.'

'Oh?' Anna's big eyes grew rounder and she felt that tears were not far away. 'I'm . . . I'm glad—for you, I mean,' she whispered, all her love showing in her expression.

Mike licked his lips, not meeting her gaze. 'I have to prove myself first, though.' Anna nodded, lost in her own thoughts. Mike was going away. Mike, the man she loved. If only she could go too! Oh, why didn't he ask her? Did he want her to wait for him, or . . . ? Or was this an excuse to finish a relationship from which he was getting so little?

Anna's lips dared not frame any of the questions her heart was asking. She was so afraid of the answers.

Mike cleared his throat and, with eyes suspiciously bright, Anna raised her face, prepared to hear the worst. 'I have to prove myself by going to their Northern Ireland factory. Just to show I'm made of strong stuff!' he joked, and Anna gasped.

'Mike! You can't! You . . . ' her voice trailed off.

'I know, Anna. I know,' Mike's arms went around her again, and wearily she rested her head on his shoulder. 'Don't worry about me. I'll be OK. And when I get back I'll have a better job, better prospects. Might even become Deputy Area Manager,' he whispered. 'Area Manager's wife, Anna. You'd like that, wouldn't you?' he coaxed, and relief shot through her. He wasn't trying to ditch her!

'Mike, I don't care about promotion. I would marry you tomorrow if . . . if you asked me,' she hurried on, blushing at her own cheek.

He sighed. 'Look, Anna. I haven't anything to offer you. When I return things will be better. I could get a bigger flat for one thing.'

She shook her head, smiling a little as she planned for their future. 'Silly, a Deputy Area Manager ought to have a house. Three bedrooms and a nice big sitting-room,' she added, thinking of the children she and Mike would have. 'Of course I would have to qualify first. You won't mind, will you?' she asked, afraid that he wouldn't let her continue her training.

'No, I don't mind, pet,' he said quickly. 'Two incomes are better than one.'

'Just for a while. When the babies come I'll stay at home. No dumping them in the crèche and going back to work part-time!' Anna said firmly, and Mike flinched.

'Let's not get too domesticated!' He laughed, but it had a hollow ring to it and Anna judged that Mike didn't care for babies.

Few men did, she supposed, until they fathered their own. It wasn't necessarily a fault, though if he was really dead-set against children she would have to sacrifice her maternal longings. It was little enough for the man she loved.

Sadly, she ran her finger gently across his lips. 'When do you leave?'

He started. 'Oh, not for a few weeks. Though the call could come at any time,' he added quickly. 'Anna—do you love me?'

'You know I do! At least, I thought you did!' How could he *not* know?

'If you love me, then let me spend my last few weeks with you, love,' he whispered against her hair.

She began to protest, knowing how impossible his suggestion was. 'No, Anna, let me finish. I've got this flat to myself. I move in on Saturday. You could help me move in, share Saturday with me. It . . . it would make me so happy, Anna.' His usually arrogant voice was humble for once, and Anna hesitated.

She was off on Saturday, as he well knew. His suggestion was that they spend the whole day making love. He didn't need her help with moving—he had no furniture of his own. He wanted *her*, loved her, and was what he was asking so much? She'd said she would marry him tomorrow, so why was she hesitating? What was she saving herself for? Some handsome consultant? Or a senior registrar with a steady gaze that burned right through to her soul?

With a frightened gasp, she broke away from Mike. She didn't want to make the decision. And, try as she might, she could not shake off the image of penetrating blue-grey eyes staring accusingly at her, waiting for that decision.

CHAPTER FIVE

'ANNA?' Mike's voice was rough with emotion, and she put out a hand to ward him off, even though he hadn't moved.

The decision was made. If she loved him she had no choice. If she turned him away now he would find solace in the arms of some pretty Irish girl. He might not even wait that long, she thought wryly. She had to prove how much she loved him and in Mike's opinion there was only one way to do that.

Her voice was steady as she gave him her answer. 'Yes, I'll help you move in on Saturday. You were wanting to show me your new flat, weren't you?'

'Anna! You really mean that?' Mike seemed unable to believe his ears and Anna smiled sadly. He hadn't expected her to capitulate, then.

After a long, lingering kiss they made plans to meet on Saturday morning then Mike strolled away, whistling.

She watched his powerful figure until he was lost in the darkness, then she shivered, the cold and damp easing their way through to her very bones. The die was cast and after Saturday there would be no going back.

But what, she wondered, was she going to tell Mother?

Friday passed slowly for Anna. She spent the morning in a daze. She changed her mother's library books then, greatly daring, popped into a quaint fifteenth-century café for elevenses, even though coffee and biscuits awaited her return home.

I'm tired of coffee and biscuits! she thought, rebelliously. The biscuits at home were always the same, wheatmeal without even a trace of chocolate. She settled herself in the window-seat so that she could watch the passers-by as they made their way to the big market. She ordered hot chocolate and fresh scones which, when they came, were running with butter and honey.

With a sigh of contentment, she made inroads on a scone, idly watching the main street. It was Middleborough's only street of any length, and ran from the market, past the small council estate and the bus depot, finishing up at the school. The shops in the town were spread out, which helped to give the area character, she thought. True, there were a couple of supermarkets, but no big shopping precinct.

Anna finished her scone and was debating whether or not to eat the second one when she saw a familiar figure pass by. Dr Rick Alexandre—and he wasn't alone.

She pressed her face closer to the window, anxious to see who the woman was before the couple passed from sight, but she was too late. She was left with the impression that his companion was tall and blonde, but she didn't think she knew her. She didn't know any tall blondes except Staff Nurse Powell and it was unlikely that she appealed to Dr Alexandre. He would go for the more elegant, sophisticated type, Anna judged.

Smiling sadly, she finished her drink and hurried away, her appetite gone.

After lunch Anna sat deep in thought, her romantic novel unopened on her lap. Tonight there was a party in the Nurses' Home. They had great parties there or so she'd heard. Not that parties appealed much but neither did sitting at home reading to her mother, or running errands for Mrs Jenkins and Nurse Dixon.

Idly, she glanced at the cover of her novel. It was a light Regency romance, set in the days when men were men and women did not need to masquerade as men, claiming equal opportunities, insisting on paying a half share on an evening out. Strange, she peered more closely at the hero on the cover, he resembled Dr Alexandre, though she could not see what colour his eyes were. The profile was the same. The strong nose, firm jaw, dark hair . . .

Mike. She ought to be thinking about Mike. *He* was the man she loved. She couldn't have Dr Alexandre, nor indeed did she want him. He was too changeable, blowing hot and cold without rhyme or reason. No, Mike was a good man. One day he would be a good husband, she supposed.

Thoughts of marriage reminded her of tomorrow. Saturday. The day she would find out what being a woman was all about. Anna's hands felt clammy and she wiped them on the tartan rug covering her knees. It was cold on the verandah but it was the only place she could be alone with her thoughts. What would Mike's love-making be like, she wondered. Just the thought of it frightened her. Twenty-one and she'd never been to bed with a man! How the younger students would laugh. On her first ward there had been a pupil nurse who continually boasted about her sexual experiences. Anna recalled how this girl had jeered at another student when the student admitted that she'd never had intercourse.

Anna coloured. She felt feverish and apprehensive. She pressed her clammy hands to her burning cheeks. How would she cope? Would Mike make allowances for her inexperience? Questions went around and around her brain, making her dizzy. Well, tomorrow she would find the answers to those questions. And the prospect terrified her.

'Anna!' Mrs Jenkins' soft Welsh voice came from somewhere within the house and Anna was glad to get away from her nightmare thoughts.

'Ah, you're here then!' Mrs Jenkins sounded delighted and Anna smiled. She liked the house-keeper and only wished Nurse Dixon was more like her. Then her smile faded as her troubled eyes met Dr Alexandre's.

Her fever vanished and she felt cold all over. 'Is . . . is something the matter, Doctor?' she asked, rising.

The registrar's eyes rested on her thoughtfully, and she had the urge to back away. 'No, there's nothing wrong, Anna. I came to fix up about tomorrow.'

'Tomorrow? That's Saturday,' she said foolishly.

'So it is, so it is,' he murmured, smiling his thanks at Mrs Jenkins, who bustled away.

Now they were alone, Anna didn't know what to say to him. She'd heard men preferred girls who listened, so she remained silent. If he wanted to make conversation, that was up to him. Saturday was the day she was going to belong to Mike Forster and Dr Alexandre had no part in it.

But what, a voice whispered, if it was Rick Alexandre and not Mike Forster? Wouldn't tomorrow be a day of rejoicing? Would you feel the same fear, the apprehension?

'No!' she said aloud, answering the voice, then bit her lower lip when she realised what she'd said. It was true. Those blue-grey eyes were beautiful. They *were*. It wasn't just her imagination. He had long dark lashes and those big eyes with their steady gaze. And the way his eyes crinkled at the corners when he laughed was really fetching.

Her lips moved but no sound came as realisation dawned. She was infatuated with this man! That was the reason he was never far from her thoughts. It was *his* face, *his* eyes, that hovered before her when she ought to have been concentrating on something else.

'Do you usually make faces at guests or am I especially privileged?' Dr Alexandre asked, his eyes watchful now.

With an effort Anna pulled herself together, the enormity of her discovery causing her to speak sharply, 'I was *not* making faces, Dr Alexandre! And as I'm off duty tomorrow, I don't see that we have anything to discuss.'

'I see,' he said agreeably, settling himself in the wicker armchair Anna had just vacated. 'Bit nippy out here, isn't it? No central heating?' He gazed up at her, eyes innocent.

He must never know how she felt! But how could she hide it? He mustn't see her face, it was like an open book. Swiftly, she crossed to the verandah windows and looked out at the long garden with its denuded trees. 'What is happening on Saturday?' she asked, her voice muffled.

'Ah, yes. Saturday. It's my day off as well as yours,' he said, and Anna waited, wondering if he had some task he wanted her to perform for the hospital.

'Is it carol-singing?' she asked hopefully. She enjoyed singing but it seemed a bit early.

'Christmas isn't quite ready to descend upon us, Anna. I thought we might go for a drive,' he went on equably. She swung round to face him.

'Go for a drive?' she echoed. 'With you?'

'Mm. A nice idea, don't you think?'

Anna shook her head. 'Why do you want to take me for a drive? Isn't your blonde friend available?' she asked tartly, and he looked astonished.

'Which blonde friend? Let me see now.' He began ticking off names on his fingers, still with that infuriatingly smug expression on his face. 'There is Angela—no, she's more of a reddish-brown. Then Olivia—no, she isn't blonde any more. Or what about Betty? I don't think so—haven't seen her lately. I've got it! Must be Simone—she was blonde last time I saw her.'

'Dr Alexandre,' Anna said patiently, 'I do not want a rundown of all your girl-friends. I'm sorry Simone and Betty and . . . and Oliver can't make it but I'm not substituting for them.'

'Olivia, dear, not Oliver. You'll get me a bad name!' he drawled, and Anna exploded.

'For pity's sake, leave me alone!' she cried, turning away so that he should not see her distress. '*Please* go home!' She bit her lip savagely, and tasted the saltiness of her own blood. Tears pricked her eyes, she wanted to fling herself on to her bed and bawl her heart out. Oh, why didn't he go!

'Home is in Jersey, Anna,' he said, from just behind her, and she started visibly. 'Home can be wherever you want it to be, though,' he went on, his voice a murmuring caress, and Anna felt his warm breath on the back of her neck.

Irritably, she turned up the big collar of her thick-knit sweater. She didn't want him breathing on her. She wanted no part of him. In fact, she hated him at that very moment. He had no right to invade her home, tormenting her, driving her out of her mind.

Strong, lean hands turned down her collar, and his thumb caressed the nape of her neck. She almost groaned aloud but years of self-discipline paid off, and she stood, seemingly unmoved by the gesture.

With a chuckle, Rick ran his fingers through her luxuriant curly hair, and she could not suppress the tremor that shot through her body, starting at her head and spreading down to her toes. When his lips gently nuzzled her ear and neck, she tensed, wanting to break free but knowing she could not.

She bit her lip again, praying for strength. She would *not* respond to his love-making. He was simply toying with her like a cat with a juicy mouse. He wasn't serious. He couldn't want her. He had so many others, Anna felt sure. Anyway, tomorrow was *her* day. Hers and Mike Forster's. If only she could hang on to that thought, it would help her now to fight off this other man's attraction. She was slowly coming under Rick Alexandre's spell. But she mustn't!

His hands moved and settled around her neat waist, his arms holding her fast, while his mouth wandered ceaselessly—over her face, her eyes, her ears.

Her heart was doing crazy things now, a wild jungle dance, she thought. Her legs were no longer her own. She didn't know if she *had* limbs left, her bones were turning to water and her pulses quickened even more. There was a strange liquid feeling somewhere in the region of her abdomen. She had never felt like this before. Poor Mike was a beginner compared with this man.

She ought to protest, break away, scream for Nurse Dixon even. She ought to but she could not. Her senses flamed anew as he turned her towards him and cradled her face in his strong hands.

'Look at me, Anna,' he commanded, and she obeyed, seeing him only through a mist of tears. 'Anna,' he groaned, drawing her close. His dark head bent to hers and, without conscious effort on her part, Anna's mouth came up to meet the insistent demand of his.

He was kissing the corner of her mouth when a shocked Mary Dixon found them. Anna, bemused and feeling in seventh heaven, glanced over at the nurse without surprise. It was inevitable that they should be found out. Such pleasures were for other girls. She knew hers would be snatched back by their rightful owner before she could enjoy them.

Mother would be told and would cause a scene. Dr Alexandre would flounce off in a rage and within a few hours the story would be all over the hospital. The mother of that big student nurse Curtis didn't allow men to kiss her daughter!

Sadly, she pushed Rick away, feeling bereft once she was out of the shelter of his arms. 'Yes? Does Mother want me, Mary?'

Mary Dixon's face was a study, her prominent eyes almost standing out on stalks, the better to get a good view of Rick Alexandre. 'I . . .' she began, then recovered swiftly. 'Your mother sent me to ask who your visitor was, Anna. Mrs Jenkins told her it was a young man and Mrs Curtis was surprised.'

Surprised wouldn't be the word, Anna mused wryly. Stunned and infuriated might be nearer the truth. 'I'll see my guest out, then pop in to see Mother,' she said firmly, unwilling to introduce the registrar.

Affronted, Mary Dixon walked starchily away, and Anna turned apologetic eyes on Rick, knowing that he was laughing to himself. 'I'm sorry, but I have to see to my mother, Dr Alexandre,' she said, with a bright smile. Her cheeks were still flushed from his kisses and she just wanted to die. He must be enjoying himself immensely, she thought, bitterly, as, still smiling, she showed him out.

It was a big house, the hall itself as large as a room. They stood side by side, the tall attractive registrar with the compelling eyes, and the slightly shorter curvy redhead, her green eyes bright with the tears she dared not shed in his presence.

Gently, Rick trailed one finger down the side of her face. 'I'll pick you up tomorrow morning, Anna,' he said, quietly. And when she opened her mouth in surprise, he kissed her briefly then let himself out, the massive oak door crashing behind him.

Anna stared at the closed door for nearly a minute, her brain refusing to function, her heart and mind unable to believe what he'd said. He was still going to take her out tomorrow! He wanted *her* company! It was incredible, unbelievable.

Yes, it was unbelievable. There was only one thing he wanted from Anna and it wasn't her sweet smile! Redheads had a reputation for being sexy which, in Anna's case, was undeserved. He probably reckoned he was on to a good thing. Maybe he thought she would be so overwhelmed that a doctor was taking an interest in her that she would let him do anything he wanted with her.

Well, Dr Jerseyman, you've met your match! She vowed silently. There couldn't possibly be any other reason for his taking her out, she accepted ruefully, settling herself in one of the easy-chairs which helped make the hall a cosy place to sit. Idly, she stared down at the patterned carpet. It was an intricate pattern—squares of deep blue and green criss-crossed by a golden wheat design. A rich, thick carpet, now a little threadbare in places. She noticed one slightly worn patch, and made a mental note to tell Mrs Jenkins. It wouldn't do if Mother saw it first.

Mother! Heavens, she'd forgotten her. All she could think about was the devastating Dr Rick Alexandre. He filled her heart and mind, her thoughts.

She hurried to her mother's room on the ground floor, still puzzling over her feelings for Rick Alexandre.

Jennifer Curtis was tight-lipped, her fine porcelain-like skin even paler than usual. 'What took you so long, darling? Was your visitor so important?' She patted the footstool beside her chair and Anna obediently sat down, her thoughts far away from the cloying atmosphere of the sick-room.

She turned sad green eyes upon her mother, knowing her dreams would soon be crushed. 'It was one of the doctors from St Aidan's, Mother. I wasn't expecting him. It's ridiculous really,' she went on sadly, 'he wants to take me out tomorrow as we are both off duty.' Dejectedly, Anna waited for the explosion, or the sobs from her mother, but strangely there were none.

'Is he nice?' her mother asked casually, and Anna shot her a puzzled glance.

'He's pleasant, if that's what you mean. At least, he is sometimes,' Anna amended, smiling a little. Sometimes he was very, very nice and sometimes he was absolutely horrid. 'He comes from Jersey,' she added.

'Does he? I spent a holiday there once. Overcrowded. Full of tourists,' Jennifer put in. 'But the scenery was breathtaking, and the food was out of this world! Will he be going back there to work?' she asked sharply, and Anna shrugged.

'How should I know? He's only just come to these parts so I expect he'll be here a couple of years. After that he might go up to London to gain more experience.' Yes, even before she finished her training he would be gone, leaving only bitter-sweet memories behind. Anna wanted to cry, and stared at her own feet rather than meet her mother's penetrating gaze.

'If he seems trustworthy *and* he is a doctor, I don't see why you shouldn't go out with him,' her mother said unexpectedly, and Anna's head shot up in amazement. 'Anna! You're crying!'

'No, no. My eyes are tired—I've been reading too much,' Anna assured her. 'Do you really mean that? You don't mind being left alone all day?'

'Of course I mind, but I'll have Mary,' Jennifer said brightly. 'Oh, no, I forgot. It's her day off. But don't worry, I'll manage. Mrs Jenkins will be here all morning.' Jennifer clasped her hands together, then twisted her wedding ring around and around her finger in an agitated gesture that Anna knew so well.

'It's all right, Mother. I'll stay. You can't be left alone all day.' Anna rose, then kissed her mother's thin cheek, trying not to show her resentment. She could not leave her alone all day to go joy-riding with Rick. It would be different if she had to go on duty but this was a pleasure trip. It was out of the question but it had been kind of Mother to suggest that she had a day out.

Tomorrow would have been a wonderful day but there was no future for her with Rick. He was at a loose end and for some reason had decided that Student Nurse Curtis would do to keep him company. Anna didn't dwell on the subject any more. She could hardly bear to think of what might have been.

After a night full of strange dreams, Anna felt washed out the next morning. Monsters and laughing, disembodied voices had filled her dreams though now she remembered only snatches of her brain's nocturnal activity.

Although she didn't feel like it, she knew she must study. So, after helping her mother to wash and dress, and settling her in the bright sitting-room, Anna gathered her textbooks and made herself comfortable in what had been her father's study. It was warm and cosy and she soon felt her eyes closing. Indeed, she was fast asleep when the door bell rang and the first she knew of her visitor was when lips brushed across her cheek.

She grimaced, thinking it was an insect, then a husky chuckle brought her wide awake. Rick Alexandre stood over her, attractive in casual clothes, his dark hair windblown, his eyes meeting her own, holding them so that she could not glance away.

'If we're having just the morning out, we ought to get cracking,' he said softly, with that lazy smile that deepened the lines of humour on his tanned face.

'I . . .' Anna began, believing him to be part of a dream. Senior registrars didn't take first-year student nurses out. It *was* a dream. It had to be.

'Come on, lazy-bones!' Effortlessly he plucked her from the chair, swinging her high in his arms, then held her closely against his chest, where Anna got a close-up of his craggy face, those compelling eyes . . .

'I . . . I can't go!' she wailed. 'Mother mustn't be left alone all day. I'm . . . I'm sorry.' Her voice trailed off forlornly, and his glance sharpened.

'Poor little Cinders. I've told your mother we shall be back directly after lunch so she won't be alone for more than an hour or so.'

'You've seen her? And she didn't mind?' Anna asked wonderingly, hope glowing in her eyes.

Swiftly, Rick's lips touched hers. 'She doesn't mind. She has decided I'm respectable!' he chuckled. 'Get your coat and we'll be off.'

Still not quite believing him, Anna rushed to get her anorak, then glanced with dismay at the jeans she was wearing. If he was taking her to lunch she must wear a dress. Having no social life, Anna possessed very few dresses. Frantically, she rummaged in her wardrobe. The choice was between a deep green woollen dress and a beige suit. Neither of them looked right but in the end she settled for the dress, since the registrar was casually dressed. The suit was perhaps rather too dressy.

Making a note to buy herself some new clothes, Anna flew downstairs.

Her mother's door was ajar and Anna hesitated before pushing it open.

CHAPTER SIX

JENNIFER was sitting in the wing-backed chair by the fire and she smiled as Anna moved nervously forward, 'What a delightful young man, Anna! He was so charming.'

Anna felt the tension ebb out of her. 'Do you like him?' she asked, deliberately keeping her voice non-committal. This about-face of her mother's was too sudden to last.

'Mm. Those eyes! Rather like your father's,' Jennifer went on, staring into the flames.

'Are they? I thought Father's eyes were green,' Anna mused. 'Dr Alexandre's are blue-grey,' she went on, forgetting to guard her tongue.

'You noticed, then?' her mother said sharply, and Anna blushed. 'Don't get involved with him, pet. He won't stay at St Aidan's for ever and I couldn't bear to lose my little girl!'

'We won't be long, Mother. He's sure to bring me back early. He will want to do something more exciting with his afternoon and evening,' Anna assured her before slipping out.

Perhaps the blonde she'd seen him with yesterday was booked for the evening. Where would they go, she wondered, as she walked sedately out to the big bronze-coloured car.

'Thought you'd had second thoughts,' Dr Alexandre said mildly, settling a rug about her and tucking it around her knees.

She tensed as his hand settled on her knee, then he chuckled and removed his hand, and Anna felt embarrassed. He thought her strait-laced and old-fashioned, she could see it in his eyes.

Mike never treated her that way. He accepted . . . Mike! She groaned aloud. Mike was moving house today and she'd promised to be with him! She'd completely forgotten him!

The registrar took no notice of her groan and might not have heard it. Apparently he expected no small-talk from her, and for once she was glad he thought her a provincial miss. No way could she conduct a conversation at that moment.

Mike. Where would he be? They had arranged to meet beside the clock-tower at eleven. He knew she might be late so would probably hang about for her. Quickly she glanced at her watch. Five past ten. He wouldn't be there yet.

With a sigh of relief she settled back. She didn't know how she was to escape from Dr Alexandre but she must, somehow. Time enough to worry about that later. He must not suspect anything was amiss.

'In a hurry, Anna?' a mocking voice asked, and she jumped.

'Oh, no, no! I just wondered what time it was,' she lied, feeling guilty for lying and hating him because of it.

'Not meeting anyone, are you?' he asked perceptively, his tone sharper now, and wildly Anna denied it.

'I suppose you have to be secretive. Your mother keeps you on a tight rein, doesn't she?' he went on reflectively, and Anna began to protest.

'No, of course she doesn't. But she's lonely, and I *am* her only child. She ought not to be left alone too long, Doctor. We . . . I mustn't be late back.'

'Rick, not Doctor!' he snapped. 'And I have already promised to return you safe and sound by one-thirty. Unharmed and untouched,' he added dryly, and her control snapped.

'There's no need to be so . . . so patronising!' she said tightly. 'I'm not a little girl!'

'Your mother treats you like one, though.' When she didn't reply, he snapped, 'Well, doesn't she? Answer me, Anna!'

'Yes, she does!' she said, then hastily averted her face so that he should not see the tears. They were tears of self-pity, she knew. Weeping because at twenty-one she was still treated like a child. Anna Curtis, you ought to be ashamed of yourself! she told herself silently.

'I thought we would take the coast road,' the registrar went on, his voice gentle now, but Anna wasn't deceived.

He had a diabolical temper and she wondered why she had ever believed him to be good-humoured.

Anxious to forestall any more questions about her mother, Anna began to talk about the hospital, but got only non-committal replies from Rick, sometimes a grunt, so she gave up. It was fine by her if he'd become bored by her conversation—and her company.

The sea was calm, a dark blue-grey, and Anna couldn't help making a comparison with the registrar's eyes. Stormy-grey, tranquil on the surface but with hidden, dangerous undercurrents.

They stopped for lunch just outside Southampton, at an impressive hotel. Anna felt her
courage fail her—and her appetite left as well. It
was just after twelve. She was one hour late for her
assignation with Mike. What must he be thinking?
That she'd been unable to escape from her mother
and that she didn't love him enough to even try?
He might be worried, thinking she'd had an accident. No, Mike never worried. It was alien to his
nature.

Stern eyes focused on her, and Anna saw a
muscle twitch at the corner of Rick's beautifully-
shaped mouth. 'Your body appears to be here but
where is the rest of you?' he asked bitterly.

Impulsively, Anna put her hand over his as they
relaxed with their pre-lunch drinks, her big eyes
begging him to understand. 'Please, R . . . Rick.'
She blushed as she used his Christian name. 'Please
. . . I'm sorry I'm not very good company. I have a
lot on my mind.' She tried to send him a silent
message, willing him to understand and make
allowances but he seemed not to read what was in
her eyes.

He moved his hand, and stared moodily into his
Martini. Anna, feeling she'd been slapped, sat back
in her chair, her eyes once more on the clock just
behind Rick's head. Twelve-fifteen. What was
Mike doing now?

She realised now that she didn't particularly want
to spend the morning with Mike. Certainly she did
not want to spend it in his arms. She wanted to be
with Rick Alexandre. It was guilt that made her
long for the outing to be over. She could not enjoy
herself knowing that Mike was somewhere out

there, waiting on a chilly street corner, waiting in vain for a girl who professed to love him.

'Have you time for lunch?' Rick asked, icily polite, and Anna clenched her fists under the table.

'You needn't be so hateful,' she muttered, knowing she deserved his contempt.

'Presumably you're anxious to return home, tail between legs like a naughty puppy, so I won't keep you long.' This cold voice wasn't coming from Rick surely?

Heartbroken, she assured him that she was looking forward to her lunch.

'Good. So am I.' His speech was clipped. 'The food will take my mind off the indifferent company!'

'Why, you . . . you . . .!' Anna's voice trailed off as she glared at him across the expanse of starched white tablecloth. 'That was uncalled for!'

'Was it?' he asked bitterly. He ordered for them both, after enquiring uninterestedly what she wanted. 'We had better make this a quick meal as my company is so boring,' he carried on conversationally. Anna's fingers closed around the handle of her knife.

'Are you usually violent?' He sounded interested, as he leaned forward. Anyone watching would have taken it for an intimate gesture as his strong hand closed over Anna's, prising the knife away.

Only Anna saw the storm signals in his eyes, knew that only the crowded restaurant was keeping him from dealing out swift retribution. That retribution would come, once they were alone, and her heart fluttered. It was half fear, half excitement. Rick was a dangerous man to cross, despite the pleasant exterior he presented to his senior colleagues.

The arrival of their soup precluded further thought, and Anna got through it as quickly as she could without appearing gluttonous. It was delicious mushroom soup, and to her surprise Anna found no difficulty in finishing it. But solid food was a different matter. Her mind was too active, her thoughts too overwrought for her to digest a meal, and she only picked at the main course, *Coq au Vin*. The chicken was tender but her poor brain couldn't send the right messages to her hands and she pushed it away after a few mouthfuls.

The pudding was more easily disposed of—a creamy meringue with fruit, and she managed to eat half. Her mouth was dry and she drank readily of the wine Rick put before her, only half aware that he merely sipped his and did not refill his glass.

'Not quite one o'clock,' he commented as they finished, but Anna already knew the time. Hadn't her frightened gaze been on the clock all the while they were eating?

'Quickest off-duty meal I've had for some time,' he went on, helping her into her coat. He led her out to the car and fastened her seat belt for her.

The big car moved out into the heavy traffic and she sat, head turned away from him. She couldn't look at him, she couldn't! What would he say to her, do to her? How angry he must be! All that money on a meal and she'd wasted half of it. And the wine she'd drunk! Registrars didn't earn all that much, she supposed. He must be infuriated because he had wasted his hard-earned cash on her.

Anna wasn't drunk but had imbibed enough to make her feel light-headed, not of this world. She would repay him. She had enough money with her. Indeed, she'd brought out quite a lot of money, believing she and the registrar would share the cost of the meal. Men did not, she felt sure, take girls to expensive hotels or restaurants without expecting something in return.

She could not give this man what she had intended giving Mike, but she could reimburse him. Still feeling light-headed and rather weary, Anna emptied out the contents of her red leather purse on to her lap and gazed at the coins in puzzlement. It wouldn't be any use giving him coins, would it? No. She shook her head and reached inside the wallet compartment. Ah, that was better. She extracted a five-pound note and examined it carefully. Yes, the metal strip was intact and the note wasn't torn. That should be enough for the hurried meal.

She could not remember how much wine she'd had. She recalled having her glass refilled at least once. Then there was the pre-lunch drink. Perhaps another pound? Feeling that it wasn't quite adequate but not wanting to ask him to change another five, she held out the money and smiled, hesitantly.

'Is that a tip, Anna?' he asked, his eyes going back to the road.

She looked down at the money and tried to remember what it was for. 'No, it's for the drink. Oh, and the chicken,' she finished, pleased that she had remembered.

Seeing that he was fully occupied with the lunch-time traffic, Anna carefully folded the notes several times and tucked them into the breast pocket of his tweed jacket.

'Thank you,' he said, pleasantly enough, and she sank back against the leather upholstery and closed her eyes. She had done her duty. Rick had been repaid. Now they could go home.

'Anna!' Roughly, she was shaken awake, and a strong light hurt her eyes.

She rubbed her eyes, then shook her head, trying to clear it, but the fuzziness persisted. 'Are we there?' she asked hesitantly, and the registrar grunted.

'I suppose that means yes,' she said irritably, as she uncurled herself from the front seat, and felt the doctor's hand on her arm as he urged her forward.

The bungalow swam before her eyes, and the fuzziness cleared. She didn't live in a bungalow!

She turned puzzled eyes on her companion. He still had an angry, set expression on his face, and she trembled. 'Where are we?' she asked hesitantly, afraid of sparking off another argument.

'This is my bungalow. I stay here when I'm off duty.'

'Oh! It's very nice,' she said cautiously. 'Can we go home now? Mother mustn't be alone too long.' She pulled back her sleeve so that she could see her wrist-watch. 'Rick! It's twenty past!'

'Is it?' He made a great show of consulting his leather-strapped watch. 'Yes, you're right. That gives us ten minutes then.'

He unlocked the front door and stood aside for her to enter. 'Ten minutes for what?' She clung to the car, unwilling to be forced into the bungalow.

'Ten minutes for me to extract a full confession from you!' he snapped, moving towards her. Nervously, she followed him inside.

'There! Make yourself at home, Anna!' He disappeared, and Anna gazed around. The fresh air had sobered her, but her head was splitting and she hoped Rick was providing strong coffee.

The sitting-room was small, much smaller than her own, but had a homely, lived-in air. The chintz settee on to which he'd deposited her was a big one and long enough for her to stretch out her aching legs. Idly her eyes took in the rest of the furniture as she waited for whatever the registrar had in mind.

There were two matching armchairs and she was almost sure that the armchair opposite had winked at her! Foolish girl. She sat up just as the coffee appeared. Rick had shed his jacket and she had a close view of a brown, polo-necked sweater and tight-fitting black trousers, as he placed the tray on the small table by the settee.

'That smells good,' she said meekly, as he handed her a cup.

He shot her a guarded gaze from under lowered brows. 'Not trying to escape then? We aren't far from the local police station. You could always sob out your story to the cops.'

'I'm glad you told me. I might just do that!' she snapped, all her new-found meekness dissolving. 'Mother will be crying very shortly. She always does when I'm late. But you don't care, do you?' she stormed, springing up and beginning to pace up and down in front of the imitation log-fire. 'It doesn't bother you that she's a sick woman and I'm all she has left!'

He shook his head, smiling a little, and she longed to wipe the smile off his face. 'You're old enough to take care of yourself. There's no need for your mother to worry about you. Certainly you're *big* enough to take care of yourself,' he added nastily, and Anna flushed.

'Anyone would think I was an Amazon!' she flared.

'They were even bigger, weren't they?' he asked, sounding genuinely interested, and Anna bit her tongue, trying not to retaliate.

'I'm five feet eight,' she said at last. 'I weigh nine stone and I take size five and a half in shoes. My statistics are thirty-eight, twenty-four, thirty-seven. I'm not *that* large!'

'Surely you're more than thirty-eight?' Lazily he smiled up at her. 'Around the breasts, I mean. When I did a mental estimate of your vital statistics, I thought about forty inches,' he said, conversationally.

Anna was speechless, and he chuckled. 'I won't bore you with my measurements. I know you aren't interested. Meeting Mike, were you?' he asked, in the same tone, and Anna almost fell into the trap.

'Mike? Oh, you mean my . . . my friend?'

'Yes, that's the one. Drink your coffee, dear,' he urged, his eyes never once leaving hers.

Frightened at his sudden change of mood, Anna gulped down the coffee, still standing by the fire. There was no escape. But what did he know about Mike?

'What time were you due to meet him?'

Innocently she smiled over at him. 'Who?'

'You kept glancing at your watch. I assumed you

had a previous engagement,' he said levelly, but Anna shook her head.

'I was worried—about leaving Mother so long, I mean,' she assured him.

'Don't give me that!' All of a sudden he was beside her, his strong fingers gripping her wrist. 'How many men are you dangling on a string?'

'None! Let me go!' Try as she might, she was unable to prise her wrist free. 'You're hurting me, Rick!'

'That's too bad. I want to hear about this Mike. Is he the one with the permed hair?'

'It is *not* permed! It's naturally curly. His hair grows that way!'

'Oh, run your fingers through it, do you? Why not try mine. It's naturally straight!' He pushed her on to one of the armchairs then sat on the arm, his body pinning her to the chair. 'Go on. Run your fingers through mine. It's free!' he invited, and Anna recoiled.

Enraged, Rick forced her fingers through his hair. The moment she felt its springiness, its texture, Anna groaned. Of their own volition her fingers carried on caressing his dark head, marvelling at the emotion such a simple act could arouse. Her index fingers caressed the nape of his neck without any directive from her, and it was Rick's turn to groan.

She found herself on his lap, with his lean face only inches from her own. Daringly, she reached up and ran her fingertips over his eyes, down his straight nose, across his sensuous mouth . . .

When his lips met hers, she offered no resistance, made no demur. This was what she had wanted from the moment they met. No wonder she had been reluctant to let Mike touch her, frightened at the idea of belonging to him. She wanted to belong to Rick Alexandre and to no other.

His kisses drugged her and combined with the wine she'd drunk—a heady combination. When he began to unzip her dress she protested, but it was a half-hearted protest, her lips barely forming the words that would deny him. This was so right! They belonged together. She loved him so it must be right.

She reached up and stroked his dear face, then a tremor shot through her as his fingers closed over her breast. 'Please don't,' she murmured. She ought to protest more vigorously, but his hands were doing crazy things to her mind as well as to her body and she had no will left to resist him.

'It's all right, Anna. Don't fight me now,' he soothed, his voice strange and husky, unlike his normal, everyday tones. 'I want you,' he whispered. 'If you're going to say no, dearest, say it now,' he said, then his teeth began to nuzzle her breast.

'No, please. I . . . I mean yes,' she murmured, her own urgency matching his. 'I love you, Rick,' she said, wonderingly, forcing open her heavy eyelids so that she could gaze into the eyes of the man she loved.

Gently, he kissed her eyes and a sweet smile curved her mouth. He loved her! Wasn't he proving it by word and gesture? This was heaven!

'How many men have you had, Anna?'

The question sobered her, and she didn't know how to answer. If she confessed her virginity he would laugh. Yet if she didn't, he would be angry, expecting an experienced lovemaker and finding only a scared, immature girl.

She forced the word out between clenched teeth. 'None.'

Rick gave a heavy sigh and Anna felt the cold at last. Her body began to shake and she couldn't control it. 'I wanted you to!' she wailed.

He got up and walked away from her, then sighed, a deep, troubled sigh, and she wanted to run to him, let him rest his dark, tousled head on her shoulder. Yet she must not.

He ran long fingers distractedly through his hair and managed a brief smile. Anna hardly dared breathe.

'I'll drive you home. Shan't be a jiffy.' He turned towards the door, then changed his mind, moving purposefully towards her instead.

She tensed, waiting for this dangerous animal to spring. Instead, he trailed his finger down her still flushed cheek. 'I know you can't help it, Anna. You didn't mean to tease.'

She gave a tremulous smile. 'I'm sorry. Really I am. I'm not like that. Not promiscuous, I mean,' she faltered, then flinched away from the laughter in his eyes. 'There's no need to laugh! I can't help the way I am!' Her voice rose, and the laughter died away from those stormy eyes.

He moved closer, then put lean, capable hands on her shoulders, his touch sending a thrill down her spine and up again. Her body pressed itself to his, and her face lifted to receive his kisses. Desire sprang between them again, and she clung to him unashamedly.

'Anna!' he moaned, then pushed her violently away. He gazed down at the stricken girl.

She couldn't meet his gaze. Embarrassment covered her. She was horrified at her own reaction. Certainly it wasn't the sort of behaviour one expected from Jennifer Curtis' daughter.

Rick chuckled, the sound making Anna wish herself dead. 'I'm surprised at you, Anna! I didn't know you were capable of such provocation!' he taunted, then he strolled towards the door whistling a little tune as he went.

CHAPTER SEVEN

THE drive home was a nightmare for Anna. She didn't know where to look, she was so embarrassed. Perhaps she'd imagined the incident. Why, it was completely foreign to her nature!

She coloured fiercely at her thoughts, wishing Rick Alexandre miles away. He must be laughing to himself! Indeed, he seemed in remarkably good humour. He was still humming a little tune. Anna could hear it above the purr of the engine.

How dared he sound so happy! She was miserable and her head ached. Her body ached too, from non-fulfilment. She wanted Rick. Her body, her senses had clamoured for him, and now she was frustrated, aching inside. It was a deep, gnawing ache such as she'd never experienced before. Was that love? she asked herself, but came up with no answer.

She had the car door open before the car had completely stopped, and darted away without so much as a backward glance. Poor Mother! She would be so distressed—and angry.

Jennifer *was* angry. But it was a cold, controlled anger. Anna's eyes went to the clock—nearly three o'clock!

'Oh, Mother! I *am* sorry! Time just flew!' Anna said lamely, taking her mother's cold hands between her own and trying to warm them.

Jennifer gazed at her reproachfully. 'It's perfectly all right, Anna. I realise your . . . young man comes before your mother.' She turned her head away and stared at the wall.

Anna felt guilty and angry, both at the same time. That Rick Alexandre! She'd like to bang his head against a wall! It was all his fault. No, that was unfair. She must share the blame—she hadn't wanted the interlude to end.

She paled at the thought. She was wicked. It was all her doing and she had no right to blame Rick. 'Please, Mother. I'm sorry. I know I'm late but Rick wanted to stop off at his bungalow and . . .'

'Bungalow!' Anna flinched as her mother swung round to face her. 'He took you to his home? Am I to understand you've been alone with him in his home?'

Anna nodded, avoiding her mother's searching gaze. 'Only for a short while, though. It's very small but quite pretty,' she added, but her mother was not to be sidetracked.

'I'm surprised at you, Anna. Next thing I know, you'll be coming in at all hours of the day and night, gallivanting about with him!'

'Oh, no, I won't!' Anna assured her. 'It's . . . it's all over. It wasn't ever a romance, really. He . . . Dr Alexandre doesn't like me very much,' she went on sadly, and Jennifer snorted.

'I suppose he tried it on and when you refused he turned nasty,' she said disdainfully, and Anna felt the shame washing over her.

'It was all that man's fault. If he comes here again, I'll wipe the floor with him!' Jennifer went on heatedly, and Anna hugged her.

'Please, you mustn't get overwrought. It wasn't

his fault. It was mine. I . . . he thought I was willing!' Anna almost sobbed, ashamed yet relieved that she'd confessed.

Jennifer sighed. 'They all do, my dear. Men are selfish, egotistical creatures. Their only concern is for their own comfort, their own needs. Your father was one in a million. You won't find another man like that.' They were both silent for a moment, thinking of the sweet, absent-minded man they'd lost.

'I had a young man once,' Jennifer went on reflectively. 'It was before I met Daddy. He was a doctor. Steamroller type. Nothing like your doctor to look at but the same personality. I *was* willing so he took what he could get then walked out,' she finished sadly, and Anna hugged her, feeling closer to her mother than she'd ever done before. Now she felt Mother would understand about Mike Forster so, hesitantly, she poured out the whole sorry tale, about Bournemouth, the short clandestine meetings outside Millstones, their love—everything.

It was a relief to get it off her chest and it did not upset or even bother her mother particularly, much to Anna's surprise. Mother was stronger than she'd realised.

'And this Mike?' her mother queried. 'Is he still waiting under the clock-tower?'

Anna smiled. 'I hope not! But I have to go round there and make sure. I must apologise to him.' She searched her mother's face for reassurance, and Jennifer nodded.

'Yes, I suppose you must. But you're sure you *are* finished with him? That it's all over?'

'Yes, I'm sure.' And she was. She wanted only Rick's arms about her, Rick's hard, demanding mouth on hers, Rick's body lying by her side . . . And that was something she would be forever denied.

'And Dr Alexandre? Tell me you've broken with him!' Jennifer demanded, and Anna's heart sank.

'Yes, I've broken with him,' she assured her mother, knowing it to be true, for why should he bother with her now? She'd unwittingly led him on. Now he knew the truth about her, knew she was inexperienced, he wouldn't touch her again. There were plenty of pretty girls at St Aidan's. He would soon forget the tall, red-haired student. He might already have forgotten, she mused sadly, as she made fresh tea for her mother. Once she was settled she would go into town and call on Mike. The poor man would be so angry and upset.

Mike flung open the door at Anna's knock, his face concerned, not angry at all, and guilt stabbed at her.

'Anna! For pity's sake! I waited over an hour!' He almost dragged her into the small, untidy flat and shut the door, still keeping hold of her arm.

His grip was painful and Anna tried to break free without success. 'Mike! Let me go! I bruise easily,' she protested, as he pushed her onto the old-fashioned settee and settled himself next to her.

'Where I'm going to bruise you, it won't show!' he assured her, and Anna felt the first stirrings of alarm. He must be thinking she'd come for the rest of the afternoon.

'No, Mike! Listen, please. I came to apologise . . .' she began, but his mouth covered hers and he began kissing her, expertly no doubt, but it left her cold. She no longer felt desire mounting as it used to. She'd since been aroused by a master, and Mike's efforts seemed clumsy by comparison.

He pressed her back against the cushions and something dug into her ribs. She could hear the settee protesting. Making a supreme effort she flung Mike's bulky body off, using her legs as well as her arms. She had the advantage of surprise—he wasn't expecting resistance.

'Mike! Please listen. I came to apologise, not to stay!' Her breasts heaved with the effort of freeing herself, and Mike's eyes were fixed on them.

His face was flushed and she didn't trust the feverish glitter in his pale eyes. 'You aren't staying?' he queried softly, and his lip curled as Anna nodded.

'Running back home to have your nappy changed, are you?' he taunted, and Anna flinched.

'That's a nasty thing to say! We . . . we had friends in this morning and I couldn't get away from them,' she lied, hoping he would never find out the truth. 'It wasn't Mother's fault, Mike.'

He grunted, still wearing that sullen expression she'd seen so often before. 'Why can't you stay now?' He patted the settee invitingly.

'Because I have to get Mother's tea. It's the housekeeper's afternoon off,' Anna said, with some relief. At least it was a legitimate excuse.

'When I'm in Northern Ireland, you will think about me sometimes, won't you?' Mike asked suddenly, and Anna felt about an inch high.

'Oh, Mike! Must you go? Do you want promotion that badly?' she wailed, feeling wicked and selfish. Who was she to deny her boyfriend what she had offered so freely to the registrar?

He shrugged and got up, stretching and yawning. 'I'm doing it for you—for us. I need the extra money and there is a big market over there. As long as you think about me sometimes, I'll be OK,' he said, a trifle wistfully. He looked so young and vulnerable that Anna's soft heart melted and she flung herself into his arms.

With a whoop of joy, Mike tightened his arms about her and began stroking her back gently, one finger trailing up and down the ridges of her spine. Then his hand cupped her breast and she pulled herself away.

To her surprise he let her go, his smile wry. 'Not good enough for mummy's little girl, I suppose? I haven't any fancy airs and graces. All I can offer is plain and simple love.'

She felt his hurt, suffered with him, but could do nothing to ease his pain. She could not, she simply could not let him make love to her. It would be a betrayal of all she felt for Rick.

Without another word, she let herself out of the shabby flat and walked thoughtfully down the lino-covered stairs. Perhaps Mike was right. Perhaps she was a snob and unconsciously did not consider Mike good enough for her. But that was ridiculous! He was a fine man despite his faults. She cared for him. She realised she no longer loved him, if indeed she ever had, but she still wanted to be friends and she was concerned about him. The weight of her guilt hung heavy about her as she began the long walk home.

*

Anna slipped back easily into the routine on her return to duty. It was as if her two days' break had never been, as if the passionate interlude with Dr Rick Alexandre had never taken place. But it had! She loved him. She was quite sure of that now, though a cautionary voice within reminded her that she'd been convinced, once, that she loved Mike Forster. Anyway, it didn't matter. Dr Alexandre would have no time for her now. Of that she *was* convinced.

It seemed that she was right. During the next few days whenever they met he was cold, distant, impersonal, as if he'd never held her in his arms.

They were perfect strangers now and it hurt. Anna still went about her duties with a pleasant smile for the patients, but the light within had died. Once off duty, she went to bed early and rose late. She hadn't the energy for anything but no one appeared to notice save Mrs Jenkins, who told her she must ask the doctor for a tonic. The doctor *was* the tonic if she but knew! It wasn't medicine Anna needed, it was a smile from the doctor, an intimate look from those beautiful blue-grey eyes.

The patients were much the same as before. John Snelling was showing signs of improvement, his diabetes was becoming more stable, and it seemed as though he would have to be discharged before Christmas.

On Dr Tester's ward-round days they were always busy and that particular day was no exception. Everyone, it seemed, was to have the big bath, and Anna was rushed off her feet.

Apart from being so depressed she was also studying hard as the notes on heart disorders for

Sister Noakes were due to be presented at the end of the week, and she was nowhere near finished, despite her valiant efforts. She simply could not study, for Rick Alexandre's lean face *would* keep getting in the way, his mocking eyes gazing up at her from her textbooks.

With a sigh, she straightened up as she finished running yet another bath. This one was for John Snelling, and she was about to call him when strong arms curled themselves about her waist.

For one heart-stopping second she thought it was Rick, and she didn't struggle, a half-smile hovering about her mouth.

Then she saw it was John Snelling, and treated him to her 'let's have no nonsense' look. He grinned, his hands locked in front of her, and she had great difficulty in prising them apart.

Luckily, she was far stronger than the slim-built John, and succeeded in releasing herself just as a stern voice spoke from the open doorway.

'Nothing better to do, Nurse?' the deep voice enquired, and Anna whirled around, scarlet-faced.

Dr Paul Tester leaned against the door, a scowl on his heavy-featured face, but after John had apologised to them both and assured the consultant that it was his fault, the scowl disappeared and Dr Tester chuckled, much to Anna's relief.

'Can't say I blame you, young man. I might try to snatch a quick cuddle myself if I wasn't a consultant!'

Leaving John without any reluctance, Anna meekly followed the tall, well-built consultant. Just outside the bathroom door he turned around for a closer look at her, and her eyes widened. Was his show of good humour only for the patient? Was this impatient, demanding man going to tear a strip off her after all?

He frowned. 'Where have I seen you before? That mop of carroty hair seems familiar.'

Anna didn't like her red locks being described as carroty but wisely refrained from saying so. 'I . . . I, er, nearly knocked you down in the car park a couple of weeks ago, sir,' she ventured reluctantly, and his face cleared.

'So you did. So you did,' he murmured. 'I remember—your pulse was pounding away! You were going to Brightling Hill, weren't you?'

Surprised, Anna nodded. 'Fancy you remembering that.'

'Hm. I'm not so old and decrepit that my memory is going,' he said dryly, and Anna laughed, her green eyes lighting up.

Realising almost immediately that she had no business smiling at consultants, Anna asked what she could do for him, and Dr Tester winked.

'Well now, that's the sixty-four thousand dollar question, isn't it!' he chuckled. 'I was looking for Sister, as a matter of fact. I couldn't see her, there was no one manning the nurses' station, so I ended up searching the bathrooms.'

'Oh, I'm sorry, sir!' Not that it was her fault, but it wasn't very nice for a senior doctor to have to winkle out junior staff because no one senior was around. 'Sister is at a committee meeting,' she explained hurriedly, 'and Staff Nurse is off, but SEN Hatcher ought to be in the office. I'll go and find her,' she offered but the consultant shook his head, still smiling.

'No, don't bother. Tell me about yourself,' he invited, and Anna's mouth opened in a big 'O' of astonishment. Consultants weren't supposed to be interested in first-year students!

'Um, there's nothing to tell, sir. This is only my second ward.' Anna stopped, wondering how much else he wanted to know.

'Enjoying Park Ward?' he asked, and Anna nodded and said 'Yes thank you, sir' very politely, wishing he would go because she knew word of their meeting would get back to Sister Noakes.

'Good, good. Perhaps you had better find Nurse . . .' Dr Tester began, then the squeak of crepe-soles heralded the arrival of the Jerseyman. Anna saw him first because she was facing the door. The set expression on his face was one with which she was all too familiar.

'Ah, there you are, Rick! You didn't tell me there was a beautiful redhead on my ward!' Dr Tester said jovially. Rick permitted himself a tight smile, but Anna could see it was an effort. He was in a temper again and for no apparent reason.

'Sorry, sir. I didn't know you were interested in large student nurses,' Rick said cuttingly, and she flinched from the look of contempt he threw her.

Dr Tester turned puzzled eyes on Anna's stricken face, then glanced at his registrar again. 'Hardly a kind remark, Rick,' he reproached, then went on to ask Rick's opinion about a patient while Anna, glad to be forgotten, crept away, trying to hide the hurt behind a professional smile.

Large student nurses, indeed! She wasn't *that* big. He made her sound six feet tall, with muscles to match! She was so distressed that at first she failed to notice Sister Noakes observing her from the office doorway. When she did, she surprised a look of dislike, almost of hatred, on the other woman's face. Sister must have arrived back when she and the doctors were standing in the middle of the ward. She would think that Anna was making up to Dr Tester—or Dr Alexandre, and Anna still wasn't sure which one Sister preferred.

'If you aren't busy, Nurse, perhaps you would make Dr Tester some tea,' Sister said, tight-lipped, and Anna hastened to obey, then remembered John Snelling.

'John Snelling is in the big bath, Sister. He's the last one. Shall I check on him before I make the tea?' Anna asked, knowing that at that moment whatever she did would be wrong in Sister's eyes.

'No, he can manage, Nurse. For heaven's sake make the tea!' Sister said crossly, her cold brown eyes fixed on Anna's flushed face. Anna was glad to hurry away. Her cap was askew again, she knew, and Sister would draw her own conclusions from that.

After that, Anna always seemed to be bumping into the consultant, both on and off the ward, and it was inevitable that word of it got back to Sister Noakes. Not that she ever said anything. She merely treated Anna to long, searching glances at times, which were very unnerving and made Anna long to have the matter out in the open. But if Sister chose not to broach the subject there was nothing Anna could do to clear the air.

Fortunately, her notes on heart diseases were well-researched and she put the subject across in an interesting way, so Sister had no cause for complaint. Anna found heart diseases of interest, anyway, and in her reading she often found little ways of helping her mother, encouraging her to take more interest in life.

Of Mike Forster nothing was said, and Anna saw no more of him, though she thought of him often, in his dingy flat with the broken settee. Was he still there, she wondered, or had the call to his Northern Ireland factory come?

The weather was cold enough here but it would be wetter over there, Anna felt sure, and she worried about him, believing he might not be warm enough or not be eating properly. She realised now that she didn't love him, that what she'd taken for love was merely a being in love with love episode. A teenage failing that was part of growing up and which had come to Anna late because of her inexperience. No, it was Rick Alexandre she loved, Rick who filled her dreams, whose face she saw and whose voice she heard even when he was far away.

Christmas was less than one week away and Anna felt lonelier than ever. She longed to spend Christmas with the man she loved and at least she was on duty for most of the festive season and expected Rick would be too. Hadn't he told her he was bringing mistletoe on to the ward? But that was ages ago, or it seemed so. He didn't care now. He knew he wasn't going to get anything for his trouble so he must be making up to some other girl. Anna only wished she knew which one.

Deep in her brown study she didn't at first hear Rick and he had to speak twice before she was aware of him. Even then, she thought him an apparition conjured up by her mind—she had wanted to see him so her mind had obligingly projected his image. Then she realised that he was really there in the flesh, and blushed because she felt he must be aware of her need for him. He looked bad-tempered, tired, too, and Anna found herself asking after his health.

Surprise momentarily replaced annoyance on his lean face, and his eyes narrowed. 'Why should you be concerned about my well-being, Nurse Curtis?' he asked, voice and eyes chilly, and Anna shivered, feeling the iciness reach out and touch her.

'I thought you looked rather p . . . peaky,' she stammered. 'There's still a lot of 'flu going around, you know,' she hurried on, wanting to stop but unable to control her tongue. 'You ought to take care. Don't overwork or . . .'

'Thank you, Dr Curtis!' he cut in, 'but I can manage without your expert advice!'

Anna closed her eyes in pain, and he was immediately contrite. His granite face softened a little, and he patted her shoulder awkwardly. 'Sorry, Anna. I guess I'm tired. Forget what I said.' He strode on, and Anna's eyes watched his tall figure until it vanished from sight.

Then, heavy-hearted, she continued her journey to the Path Lab. Her mind was on Rick, however, and she had passed the turning and gone some way towards the administration offices before she realised where she was. Dazed and angry she was about to retrace her steps, then heard her name.

'Nurse! Nurse Curtis, wait a moment.' It was Dr Tester's voice and she wondered what he'd been doing in the Path Lab, but when she turned she saw him in the doorway of the Hospital Administrator's office. The two men said goodbye and the tall consultant hurried up to Anna, who stood impatiently, wishing Dr Tester was Rick.

Would Rick look like that when he was middle-aged? Anna pondered on the thought, seeing the grey hair at Dr Tester's temples, the hairline that was receding ever so slightly, the signs of a thickening waistline. She couldn't imagine the athletic Rick ever letting himself go like that. Why, his flat belly and . . . She checked the drift of her thoughts. She mustn't think about Rick Alexandre. He couldn't care less about her.

'Why so sad, Nurse?' Dr Tester asked, matching his longer stride to hers, and Anna smiled wanly.

'I was thinking about Christmas, sir,' she murmured. 'It would be nice if everyone could be with those they love at Christmas.'

'So it would. Do you have someone to love?' he asked lightly, and Anna's smile deepened, her green eyes widening.

'I can't tell you that, sir!' she teased, and his loud, deep laugh rang out, causing several heads to turn their way. One of the heads belonged to Sheila Haggerty, and Anna smiled at her as they passed, but without really seeing her. She wasn't seeing Dr Tester, either. Her mind was on the man she loved, as usual.

Consultant and student nurse parted outside Park Ward and Anna pushed open the swing doors, the meeting with Dr Tester already fading from her mind.

She was due off at four-thirty but carol-practice had been arranged for a quarter past five so Anna obligingly worked until just after five, then hurried to the lecture hall in the School of Nursing, where the final practice was being held. Her mother knew she would be late, knew the reason why as well, so Anna felt free to linger afterwards and share a coffee with her fellow students. Now she no longer felt so much of a stranger among the younger ones. She was beginning to fit in at last. She was really looking forward to the coffee and general discussion after the practice.

Although she loved singing, Anna was sad because a certain dark-haired doctor wasn't among the choir. Most of the songsters were nurses, male as well as female, but there was a smattering of domestics, one porter who was a lovely bass, and Mr Archer, the Administrator.

To Anna's surprise, he made straight for her when, flushed and breathless, she arrived for the session.

He was a short, portly man with a mass of white hair which Anna was sure he had permed it always looked so immaculate. Although an important member of staff, he was always friendly, so she wasn't prepared for the stern look he gave her.

He manoeuvred her into a corner of the huge hall, away from the others, and Anna's eyes widened with dismay. She knew she was about to be ticked off for some misdemeanour but wasn't aware of having committed any crime.

Mr Archer's first words showed Anna where her supposed crime lay. 'Do you realise the whole hospital is talking about you and Dr Tester?'

Anna gasped, then began to protest, already

knowing by the adamant expression on Mr Archer's face that it was useless. The St Aidan's grapevine had done its work too well.

CHAPTER EIGHT

ANNA stood numbly while Mr Archer continued his quiet but stern castigation. His words finally penetrated the cloud that enveloped her, 'I realise that nurses are not angels. I've been at this hospital long enough to have the scales pulled from my eyes!' he was saying, and Anna nodded automatically. 'So if you and Dr Tester are enjoying an affair, for heaven's sake why didn't you keep it quiet?'

'But we . . .' Anna began, but Mr Archer was in full stride now. 'It's too late to keep it quiet now, Nurse. That's the pity of it. Why on earth couldn't you pick one of the junior doctors?' he asked sharply. 'A consultant has a certain reputation to keep up, even a divorced one.' Still grumbling like an old woman, the administrator moved away, leaving a stricken Anna to gaze after him.

When the conductor waved all the singers together Anna could take no more. She fled, uncaring of the eyes and pointing fingers her imagination was conjuring up.

It was a fine though cold night, and she half-walked, half-ran all the way home. She wished with all her might she'd never set eyes on Dr Paul Tester. It could only be a matter of time before the rumour reached the ears of Rick Alexandre. He had little opinion of her as it was—what would he think then?

Next morning Anna was on duty at seven-thirty

and was surprised to see Sister's figure just ahead of her in the corridor. Sister never arrived before eight, except for a consultant's round day, and even then did so rarely. There must be some trouble on the ward but Anna could not imagine what.

John Snelling had been discharged two days before, and Anna had heaved a sigh of relief at his going. Most of the others were still there, though Mr Pearson was expected to be discharged today.

Anna hoped Sister Noakes hadn't heard the rumours. Although Sister wore a wedding ring, Anna now knew that the woman's husband had been killed on their honeymoon some two or three years before. Because of that Anna no longer felt animosity towards her senior. Her soft heart could not bear to dwell on the pain and the anguish Sister must have suffered, so she went out of her way to perform little services for her. Eliza Sulu had openly sneered and called it 'touting for Sister's favour' but Anna didn't mind. As long as *she* knew why she did it, the opinion of the others didn't matter. She had only to imagine Rick Alexandre lying in a road somewhere, his body bruised and crushed, his life-blood spilling on to the ground, to feel empathy with Sister Noakes.

If Rick should die Anna didn't think she could go on living, though she knew she would have to. Perhaps, like Sister Noakes, she would devote her life to caring for others, find peace of mind in helping others to get well even if she could do nothing for the man she loved.

Anna was so preoccupied with her morbid thoughts that Sister had to raise her voice. 'Nurse Curtis! Will you pay attention!'

'Oh! Yes, I'm sorry, Sister,' Anna replied, trying to erase the image of a dead or injured Rick Alexandre from her mind.

'Sorry! You're always sorry!' Sister snapped, and Anna flinched as if struck.

She managed a weak smile despite the harsh words raining down on her. Remember her husband died before they'd had time to get to know each other, she told herself. Think of Rick. So Anna stood patiently while Sister gave a verbal list of her faults. Indeed, she heard little more than half of what the older woman was saying. Rick might as well be dead, she thought. He was gone from her forever. And once he heard the rumours, it didn't take much imagination to work out his response. He would simply hit the roof.

It occurred to Anna that Sister must have heard the rumour because she was usually pleasant to Anna. Not exactly friendly but reasonable enough. Now she paused for breath, and Anna waited to hear if there were any more faults she ought to know about.

'Haven't you anything to say, Nurse?' Sister asked, her voice now tired and dispirited, so Anna, feeling sorry for her again, gave such a saintly smile that Sister almost choked. 'Get out of my sight until it's time for the medicine-round!' she snapped, and a puzzled Anna did as she was bid.

Sister obviously preferred Dr Tester. That much was clear now, so Anna intended to do her best to push the two of them together. She liked the consultant, to be sure, but at the thought of an affair with him she balked. She preferred blue-grey eyes!

The medicine-round was a disaster from start to

finish. Students received visits from clinical instructors from time to time, although ward sisters generally resented this and maintained that ward-teaching was *their* forte whenever they could spare the time, and Sister Noakes was at loggerheads with the School of Nursing over this point. She did not like and did not willingly tolerate clinical instructors on the ward and enjoyed teaching the girls herself.

She was a good teacher, though her manner was abrupt and sometimes off-putting to nervous learners. She was taking Anna's medicine-round that particular morning. Sister would read out the medicine card, Anna would select the appropriate medicine or tablets, show the bottle to Sister, check with the Kardex that the right patient was about to receive the right medicine at the right time, then she would give it out to the appropriate patient. Sister, being in a bad mood anyway, made Anna jumpy and nervous. However sorry she felt for the woman, Anna began to wish her a million miles away.

She had to fetch a urinal for a new patient so was a minute or so late for the round, and that didn't help matters. Then at the second bed Sister mumbled the name of the tablets and Anna, mishearing, selected the wrong ones. Of course, she would not have administered the wrong tablets as the next check would have revealed her error, but from the way Sister carried on Anna felt as if she'd been caught in the act of murdering a patient!

When that was cleared up and Sister had delivered a stern warning about carelessness costing lives, Anna moved the trolley on to the next bed.

But by now her hands were shaking and she was beginning to feel like a jelly in a hot room. So much so that when she unscrewed the cap of the next bottle, which was full, some of the pills spilled out onto the open trolley, then as Sister tried to snatch the bottle from Anna's nerveless fingers, it went flying, scattering its contents over the ward floor.

'For heaven's sake girl! Can't you do anything right?' Sister snapped, forgetting or uncaring that it would upset her patients. 'I wonder if you are as slow at other things as you are here,' Sister grumbled, beckoning to SEN Hatcher to take Anna's place at the trolley.

Anna was incapable of movement for a moment, and Sister gave her a push. 'Go and sweep up! Find every pill and hurry up with it!'

Scarlet, Anna hurried to the domestics' cupboard, and almost bumped into the muscular figure of Dr Tester, who could not have failed to hear Sister's tirade.

'I'm . . . I'm so sorry!' Anna gasped, brushing past the consultant, uncaring if it was rude. He was the cause of her trouble, albeit the innocent cause. Pausing only to blow her nose, Anna reappeared, trying not to notice as Sister and consultant stood by the first bed, eyeing her disdainfully.

'Not content with scattering pills everywhere you have to push doctors out of the way as well!' Sister Noakes said. Her voice was remarkably controlled now but Anna could see she was livid. 'Well? Aren't you going to apologise to Dr Tester?' Sister demanded, and Anna did as she was bid.

The consultant gave her a rather distant smile, and Anna felt she ought to curtsy! She walked briskly towards the scene of the disaster, trying to appear as if she hadn't a care in the world. She was past caring, anyway. Sister would believe what she wanted to believe, and there was nothing Anna could do about it. Eventually, when the woman realised that the rumour was unfounded, everything would get back to normal on Park Ward. It was a matter of time, that was all.

Sister ignored Anna for the rest of the day and Anna hoped it was because her senior felt ashamed of her outburst. Ward sister and consultant had been closeted in the office for about an hour after the medicine-round was finished, and Anna believed Dr Tester must have laughed at the rumour, if indeed he'd ever heard it, assuring Sister Noakes that there was no truth in it.

But Dr Tester evidently hadn't been reassuring enough, for Sister took every opportunity to belittle Anna in front of others in the few days leading up to Christmas. How Anna managed to keep back the bitter words of reproach she never knew. Although a nurse might be asked to leave a ward if she wasn't satisfactory, Anna knew that the last thing Sister wanted was to lose her. No, that would spoil the fun. There would be no whipping-boy if Student Nurse Anna Curtis wasn't there.

One incident in particular stuck in her mind, and the pity she felt for Sister evaporated because of it. Mr Dunster, a new patient, had been prescribed an injection, one which came in powder form and needed mixing with sterile water before being drawn up into the syringe. Anna, under Sister's stern eye, searched the small drug-cupboard, but couldn't find the exact bottle. Others were stacked in neat rows and Sister assured her that they were all in order.

Anna, getting hot under the collar and feeling the now familiar nervousness returning, moved first one bottle then another. After a fruitless search she turned to the other side of the cupboard, where enemas and other external preparations were kept. The drug ought not to be there but others weren't always as careful as they might be, and there was no harm in looking.

Naturally that was wrong and Sister did not hesitate to tell her so, in front of an audience that included Eliza Sulu, who didn't like Anna. 'The bottle is where it should be, Nurse—in the left-hand cupboard,' Sister said tartly, and Anna carefully relocked the right-hand cupboard and went back to the other one, convinced that the bottle wasn't there at all.

'Come along, Nurse Curtis! The bottle *is* there,' Sister snapped. 'It's plain enough. We're all laughing at you because you can't see it.'

'I'm glad you find it amusing, Sister,' Anna said quietly, and in the following silence she could have heard a pin drop. Sister was struck dumb and even Eliza kept her mouth closed for once.

At last, after moving every bottle, she found the missing one which had been artfully stacked in the middle of a pile of drugs with similar names.

She held the bottle aloft. 'Is this the one, Sister? I'm afraid the cupboard wasn't as tidy as you led me to believe,' Anna said levelly, her heart pounding away, amazed at her own audacity.

'Yes, that's it. Perhaps you will draw up the injection Nurse Sulu?' Sister turned to Eliza, who almost snatched the bottle from Anna's grasp.

Without waiting for further instructions from Sister, Anna quietly left the clinic and headed for the sluice where she knew there were bed-pans to be tidied away—another of the jobs Sisters delighted in giving Anna. She really felt she could not take any more, and hot tears were making her eyes smart. Sister was on leave over Christmas, that was the only bright star on the horizon. By the time she returned, the silly rumour would be forgotten and everything would be as before.

Two days before Christmas, Anna called on Mike Forster, taking him a little gift. It was nothing much and she did not suppose for a moment that he had anything for her, but she wanted him to have a memento, wanted him to know she was thinking of him. Of course he might already have left for Northern Ireland, but she would call anyway.

She snuggled into her new sheepskin jacket, an early Christmas present from her mother. It was a bright but bitterly cold day and Anna was glad of its warmth. The thought of the cold reception she would get from Mike was chilling enough without the cutting wind that went right through her.

She knew Rick was working over Christmas, but afterwards? He would perhaps pop over to see his parents. Assuming he had parents. She wondered what sort of home he had in Jersey. She had read up on the island and knew the scenery was breathtaking, with sandy beaches and isolated coves, where one might wander for hours without seeing anyone. But what of the winter? She'd read that Jersey was a year-round resort, that it did not sleep once the

main season was over, but found it hard to visual-
ise. If Mother continued to improve Anna intended
to spend a short holiday there, breathe the same air
Rick Alexandre breathed, feast her eyes on the
beautiful scenery, and wonder where exactly he
lived. Who knows, she thought, I might even bump
into him out there.

Feeling guilty because she was visiting one man
whilst thinking about another, Anna tapped at
Mike's door. There was no answer at first though
she thought she heard movement within. When no
one answered the door she knocked again, harder,
and was just debating whether or not to leave the
present, a leather wallet, when the flat door opened
a matter of inches and Mike peered out.

Surprise was mingled with some other emotion
on his handsome face, and Anna began to feel
uneasy. Perhaps he'd been in the bath or, more
likely, he was entertaining a girl and she'd dis-
turbed them at an unfortunate moment.

'Oh, er, hello, Anna. Nice to see you.' Mike was
embarrassed, and some imp within made Anna
linger even though he wanted rid of her.

'I've brought you a little Christmas gift,' she said
shyly, holding out the package in its holly-covered
paper.

A long arm reached for it, Mike being careful to
block the doorway with his body. 'Thanks, Anna.
You shouldn't have! What is it?'

'The label says do not open till Christmas Day, so
you mustn't!' Anna teased. 'Have I come at a
difficult time?' she asked, and was amused to see
the brick-red colour that spread across his face.

'Er, yes. I've just had a bath. I'm not respectable.' He laughed, and Anna's lips quivered. So much for Mike's undying love!

'I'll run along then. You haven't had the call to Northern Ireland yet?' she queried as she turned to go.

'Oh, that. No.' He looked harassed and Anna didn't delay him any longer. 'Look, it'll come soon. Probably the end of January,' he called after her. 'You'll think about me sometimes, won't you?' he said plaintively, and Anna turned to face him, her eyes softening.

She could see a bit more of him now. His shirt was unbuttoned and he was minus his belt. 'Yes. I'll think about you, Mike. I still wish you didn't have to go,' she said softly.

'I love you, Anna!' His hoarse voice followed her down the stairs and she was unable to block out the sound.

She supposed in his own way he *did* care for her. He had a girl in because he needed one. It was a normal male urge and she shouldn't judge him too harshly because of it. Even Rick Alexandre had normal male urges, she reminded herself. She wouldn't think much of him if he hadn't!

Christmas Day dawned at last, though not the white Christmas she'd hoped for. She was on late-shift which pleased her, she could enjoy Christmas with the patients and join in the festivities. At home it was almost like any other day, with only the giving and receiving of presents to mark it as something different. Mrs Jenkins naturally wanted to spend the day with her own family so Anna volunteered to cook the Christmas lunch, which was only a comparatively light meal because Mother had to watch her weight. Mary Dixon was staying on as she had no close relatives, so Mother would have company while Anna was at the hospital.

The first thing she noticed when she walked on to the ward was the mistletoe. An enormous bunch was suspended over the office doorway and other smaller sprigs were set at intervals all down the ward, with a tiny sprig over each patient's bed. Anna chuckled when she saw them, then her heart fluttered when Ruth Barratt told her it was Dr Alexandre's idea.

Would the dashing doctor kiss her under the mistletoe, she wondered. She doubted it but could not help harbouring a faint hope.

She *was* kissed under the mistletoe, under the large bunch which was hanging over the office door, but the man wasn't Dr Alexandre. Anna, all unsuspecting, hastened to obey when she saw several important-looking men trooping into the office and Staff Nurse beckoning to her. No doubt they wanted coffee.

But as soon as she set foot inside the office, Dr Tester, immaculate in dark grey suit and crisp white shirt, grabbed hold of her, pulled her out into the narrow passage so that the patients could see, then soundly kissed her.

Dimly, Anna was aware of cheering, of cries of 'Go on, Doc', but disappointment soured the moment for her. Dr Tester had large fleshy lips and she did not enjoy the kiss one jot. Because he was a consultant and because it was Christmas she made no protest, even managing to respond so that she would not embarrass anyone.

Flushed, with cap askew, she laughed up at Dr Tester then heard clapping as someone behind her applauded the kiss. The faint prickle at the back of her neck warned her.

Her smile fading, she turned and met Rick Alexandre's mocking gaze. His lips were smiling as he pretended to join in the festive mood but the deep-set eyes were hostile. Anna wished she was dead. The man she loved and he hated her! She was sure of it now.

Dr Tester kissed all the nurses so at least Anna hadn't been singled out specially, but try as she might she could not forget the expression on Rick's face, the coldness of those stormy blue-grey eyes.

If it hadn't been for the patients Christmas would have been spoiled for her after that. But she threw herself wholeheartedly into the fun. The only two rather poorly patients had been moved to the side-room which women's medical had at last vacated. Anna took her turn sitting with them, holding their hands or just listening while they talked.

They were both getting on in years, at least so it seemed to the youthful Anna, and one of them, Fred Johnson, received no visitors that day because there was no public transport and his crippled wife could not afford the taxi-fare. Anna sat by him longer than she intended.

She was gently stroking his hand when a voice she knew well called her name. Glancing up, she smiled tentatively at Rick Alexandre, who gave her a brooding, considering look, then turned his attention to Mr Johnson.

Feeling snubbed, Anna kept her eyes firmly downcast while Rick chatted to the man. She knew why he'd come, for Staff Nurse Powell had earlier said how poorly the man looked. He was purplish and very weak. Anna wondered why ITU had sent him to Park Ward but supposed they knew best.

Rick finished his examination and without another word to Anna he sauntered away, white coat flapping, head bent as if in thought. Her sad green eyes followed him, the ache within her growing by the minute. If only he would ask, she could tell him that she didn't even fancy the consultant. But he'd seen the kiss and must have been aware that she had responded.

It was like a nightmare she'd had once, of being lost in a maze, each turning leading back to the beginning with no end in sight. On that occasion, Anna recalled being awoken by the alarm before she had found a way out. But this was a nightmare come to life, surrounding her like the maze and she could see no way of solving the puzzle, of finding the exit. Her head began to throb and she patted Mr Johnson's still hand.

He appeared so peaceful, snoring gently now, and Anna wished she could just drop off to sleep like that. It was something that came with old age, she supposed, like artificial teeth. Smiling at the idea of Rick displaying plastic teeth on the rare occasions he laughed, Anna rang the bell. It was time for another nurse to take over.

During the evening the carol-singers came around. These were not the hospital singers but a group from combined local charities and the League of Friends. Anna stood in the main ward just listening, the sweet singing filling her with longing. Her heart ached with the beauty of it all and her glance swept the ward, lingering on the face of each patient in turn. It was beautiful and sad at the same time. Rick Alexandre stood a few feet away, head bent, but she didn't permit her glance to linger on him. It was obvious why he was there. Margaret Warwick was in the front row of the choir. Of course she seemed to be a friend of Dr Tester's as well as Dr Alexandre's, yet it was Rick who stood there. The consultant had gone off duty.

She wondered anew about Margaret Warwick. The woman was too old for Rick she decided, but one never knew. Perhaps he enjoyed sophisticated, experienced women. He certainly didn't want a girl who was still wet behind the ears, that was for sure. A tear trickled slowly down her cheek and, surprised, Anna brushed it away. It must be the poignancy of the moment. Never would she admit it might be sorrow because the man she loved hardly noticed her existence.

When the long shift was almost over, and the ward was quiet, the lights dimmed, Anna walked softly towards the office to check the duty-sheet and a movement in the shadows caught her eye. Dr Alexandre was holding a bunch of mistletoe aloft with one hand, his other arm was very firmly around the tall but slender girl in his arms.

Anna gasped and hurriedly stifled it, but the couple were lost in their own world. For one heart-stopping moment she believed it was Margaret Warwick but as she hovered in a convenient shadow, someone put the light on in the ward kitchen, illuminating the tender scene. It was Rick all right but the girl was blonde and Anna thought it was the girl she'd seen him with before, in Middleborough.

Evidently she worked in the hospital. As she turned, laughing, Anna recognised her as one of the Path Lab assistants, Beth something-or-other.

Her heart heavy, Anna coughed to indicate her presence, then strode briskly into the office pretending she hadn't witnessed the little love scene. Her cup of bitterness was full now. Her heart was broken and completely beyond repair.

When she returned to the ward after her days off, she found that Fred Johnson had died in her absence. Although nurses were not supposed to become emotionally involved with patients Anna had been fond of the man. He was a sweetie, in some respects like her own father, who had been admired by everyone. There weren't many men left like that, she reflected, her eyes sad as she drew up an injection under Staff Nurse Powell's eagle eye.

The injection was for Mr Robards, who was far from sweet and if anyone admired him it was Mr Robards himself. Anna had met his wife briefly, a small, thin, yet energetic woman, greatly in contrast to the eighteen-stone bulk of Mr Robards. He was a fairly new admission. Anna hadn't done many injections on Park and only one on her previous ward so each one was still an ordeal. She wasn't as dextrous as some of the others and Staff Nurse's foot was tapping impatiently by the time Anna had finished drawing up the injection.

Mr Robards eyed them uneasily as they approached his bed, then his gaze swept past them. Anna glanced back, wondering what he could see that she could not. It was Dr Tester, smiling and handsome, immaculate as ever, and he was heading straight for Mr Robards's bed.

Anna, panicking, signalled her distress to Staff Nurse, who merely shrugged. Then she relented and whispered 'I'll see him off'.

Anna was so relieved that she beamed at Mr Robards, who gave her a doubtful smile in return. 'Like sticking needles into poor defenceless men, do you?' he asked, half-jesting.

'No! Injections aren't very pleasant for nurse *or* patient. I'll just draw the curtains and make you comfortable.' As she drew the bed-curtains around Mr Robards she saw the consultant and Staff Nurse deep in conversation. Then, even as she watched, they began to walk towards the bed. Her hand stilled at the last curtain and then they were upon her.

Dr Tester gave her a friendly smile and somehow Anna formed her features into what she hoped was a smile. Hopefully Dr Tester would not stay long.

He stayed long enough to witness the injection, encouraging Anna with friendly advice. Of course that made her ten times more nervous, and Mr Robards almost shot out of bed when she inserted the needle. Hastily she comforted the man, settled him down again and drew back the curtains. In her panic she had forgotten to break the needle off from the syringe and when Staff Nurse pointed it out to her rather coldly, the consultant's disapproving shake of the head did nothing for Anna's bad nerves. That was one injection she would never forget!

Dr Tester signalled to Staff Nurse Powell that he no longer needed her and, with a penetrating glance from her sharp grey eyes, she hurried away leaving a discomfited Anna to talk to the doctor.

'I have been meaning to speak to you, Anna,' he said as they strolled into the day-room, which was empty. 'It is Anna, isn't it?' he queried, his warm brown eyes fixed on her red curls. She nodded, uncomfortably aware that a first-year student nurse ought not to be having a private discussion with an eminent consultant.

She risked a glance at him, puzzled by his manner. It seemed over-friendly, comradely, as though they were not separated by several tiers in the hospital hierarchy. He passed a large, well-shaped hand across his eyes as if fatigued, and Anna felt sorry for him. 'Would . . . would you care to sit down, sir,' she ventured, and was rewarded by a smile which lit up his face, easing away the lines, making him appear younger.

He did as she suggested, stretching out his legs as he relaxed in one of the easy chairs, and Anna perched on a corner of the table where she and the registrar had played ludo.

Her relationship with Rick might well have been years ago and thousands of miles away, she reflected, her green eyes darkening with sadness.

'Got the worries of the world upon your shoulders, Anna?' Dr Tester asked softly, and she shook her head, embarrassed that he should be looking at her. She wanted to be alone with her painfully sad thoughts. Why on earth didn't the man get to the point? Then a thought struck her and she almost flinched. Was she to be turned off Park Ward? She and Sister did not get on and no doubt news of Anna's supposed misdemeanours had reached the School of Nursing. Dr Tester often took lectures over there. Could Mrs Lucas have asked him to sort out the trouble here? With a deep sense of foreboding, she asked him bluntly what he wanted.

A flicker of surprise and possibly annoyance crossed his face. 'You don't mince words do you?' he commented, then heaved himself out of the chair, crossing over to the day-room window and gazing out at the sunny but wintry day outside.

Anna waited impatiently. She, too, rose and stood, hands behind her back like a naughty schoolgirl awaiting the headmaster's judgment.

CHAPTER NINE

PAUL Tester spun round, hands in pockets, a tentative smile on his lips. 'Would you have dinner with me one evening?'

Anna showed her surprise and his smile faded. 'No, perhaps not. Lunch then, Anna?'

'I . . .' she began, overwhelmed by the invitation and wondering what he really wanted of her. He was old enough to be her father, of her mother's generation rather than her own. 'Th . . . that would be very nice, sir,' she found herself saying. 'Lunch, that is,' she added, and his smile returned.

He pushed back his slightly greying hair in a curiously boyish gesture. 'Thank you,' he said simply, then they began to discuss dates and times.

It would have to be when Anna was off duty and that presented a problem in itself. If her mother objected to the registrar she would certainly object to a much older consultant taking her daughter out. Anna knew she must lie to Mother, painful though it was, and they fixed the following Friday for their lunch.

With eyes round with astonishment, Anna watched Dr Tester stroll out of the day-room, whistling softly to himself. The kiss he had dropped lightly on her brow as he passed burned her and she could still feel it even after she went off duty.

Such things happened only in books! A senior consultant could not be interested in a very junior nurse. It was incredible. She did know that one of the consultant surgeons was dating a second-year nurse, though, so such liaisons *did* happen.

She wasn't looking forward to lunching with Dr Tester, nor to lying to her mother, but in the event she didn't have to lie. When she glanced at the duty-sheet and saw how short they were on Friday evening, she volunteered to do a split duty.

Staff Nurse's eyebrows were raised again, but she did not comment. Anna was glad that Sister Noakes had not yet returned to duty, having contracted 'flu after her Christmas holiday. It was a welcome respite for Anna, in more ways than one.

During that week she saw little of Rick Alexandre. He was working longer hours than he ought to, she knew, because the 'flu was still decimating the ranks of more junior doctors. Whenever she met him he was unfailingly polite yet distant, as if they were strangers, as if he had never held her in his arms, never kissed and caressed her.

She saw Beth, the Path Lab assistant, twice more on Park Ward. Bitterly, she watched Beth and Rick laughing together. Indeed, the only time the registrar relaxed was in the company of the pretty blonde. Anna tried hard to be glad for him but failed utterly. She was jealous. She hated to admit it, but it was true. She wanted to be the only woman enjoying his embraces, but knew that wasn't realistic. Rick needed the company of other women, needed what they were willing and eager to give him. What he did *not* need was a cold little nurse who prized her virginity above all else—or so it must seem to him.

But she didn't! She loved him and wanted to

belong to him. Given half a chance Anna would be happy to share his bed, but that chance was not forthcoming. Rick had lost interest in her and she couldn't blame him, but it hurt that he'd been interested only in her body, that he did not care for her as a person at all.

Anna took a pretty dress and different shoes with her when she went to work on the Friday. She finished at one, and dashed to the Nurses' Home to change into the dress, a new one of fine dark grey wool. It was perhaps a drab colour in itself but it showed off her red hair to advantage. She pinned on one of her mother's brooches which she'd borrowed—a big ruby set in gold—then slipped into the plain black court shoes, thankfully putting her ugly lace-ups in her bag. The shoes she'd chosen were only medium-heeled because although the consultant was tall he wasn't as tall as Rick, and she didn't want to embarrass him.

She was terribly nervous as Dr Tester's Mercedes pulled into the hotel car-park. She had met him by arrangement well away from the hospital and hopefully no one had seen her get into his car. Word of the outing must not get back to Park Ward for Sister was sure to hear about it when she returned from sick leave.

The January air was cold but crisp, with even a hint of sunshine but Anna was glad of her fur lined jacket and mittens. Dr Tester was as immaculate as ever, his dark brown suit matching his eyes. She didn't like his shirt, which was white with a thin brown stripe, nor his tie, which echoed the same theme but then he dressed to please himself, not her.

After a superb meal they relaxed in the coffee-lounge of the restaurant, which belonged to the George Hotel, a venue of quietly understated elegance—and costliness, she found, having been shocked by the price of the food.

When she had dined with Rick she had chosen all the cheapest dishes, expecting to pay half, but as her partner this time was a consultant Anna had no hesitation in choosing what she wanted. The main course had been chicken in an exotic sauce and it had left her too full to enjoy a large pudding so she'd chosen a simple mousse to finish.

Now replete, she relaxed in a cosy easy chair, her coffee on the table in front of her, a dish of *petits-fours* within easy reach. The consultant sat by her side, but not near enough to make her feel uncomfortable. The smoke from his cigar drifted past her nostrils, and she felt she could sit there for hours, warm and content, with the man she cared for by her side.

She frowned. The wine must be making her light-headed, together with the pre-lunch red Martini. He wasn't the man she loved. Dr Tester was a stranger really. She could not claim to know him at all. He was an enigma and she found she wanted to know more about him, to find out what made him tick.

That was wrong. She loved Rick Alexandre, so could not possibly be interested in another man. Then there was Mike Forster. She seemed to be collecting men just lately!

A smile crossed her lips, curving the corners of her wide mouth, and Dr Tester's sharp eyes could not fail to notice. Gently, he ran a finger along her hand up to the wrist, and she shivered, involuntarily.

'Contented, Anna?' he enquired gently, and she nodded.

'Mm. It was a superb meal, thank you. But I expect I'd better be moving,' she added.

'Why? What's your hurry? I haven't anything on this afternoon, barring emergencies. We could take a drive along the coast. Or even stroll for a while,' he offered.

'I can't. I have to be on duty at five,' she explained, and his heavy brows drew together in what appeared to be anger.

'I imagined you to be off duty, Anna. You didn't tell me you were doing a split duty.'

'I didn't think you would be interested,' she said candidly, and he chuckled, good humour restored.

'I wouldn't have plied you with wine had I known,' he commented as they prepared to leave. 'Heaven help my patients if you have to stick needles in them this evening!' he chuckled, but Anna didn't find it at all funny.

The first person she met when she returned to duty was Rick Alexandre. She had a headache. It wasn't exactly a hangover but the drink had made her feel rather woozy and, combined with her headache, she wasn't feeling at all sweetness and light. The sight of the man she loved smiling at her did nothing to help. What did *he* have to smile at anyway, she thought crossly, believing that Beth Sinclair must have put Rick in a good mood. Well, Beth Sinclair was more than welcome to him.

She was so angry that she snapped at him when

he cornered her, edging her into the ward kitchen when she would have hurried to the office.

He looked astonished at her outburst and she was immediately sorry. 'Please, Dr Alexandre, I'm rather out of sorts. Leave me alone, I've got work to do,' she called as she scurried to the office to hear the report, uncaring that he did not follow or make more effort to stop her.

Somehow the time passed, that evening and the days following flashing by as the ward became busier. Sister Noakes returned from sick leave looking pale and groggy. Her illness had sapped her strength and she no longer took pains to show Anna up, or snap at her in front of others, so that was a blessing.

Dr Tester, or Paul as she now called him, took Anna out once a week on average, and she was slowly beginning to trust him, to accept his undemanding company. She wasn't sure of her feelings for him. Certainly he caused no heart-fluttering but he was pleasant and very attentive. He always kissed her at the end of a date and she wished he wouldn't. The kisses only served to remind her of Rick, a man for whose kisses she would give a fortune.

Anna was due to finish on Park Ward in early March, and about a week before, Paul Tester became more demanding, his kisses hungrier. To her own surprise she at first responded, thinking to forget Rick Alexandre.

Snuggled up against Paul's shoulder one wintry evening she almost forgot that he wasn't the man she loved. Since Rick no longer cared, Anna tried to assuage the hunger she felt for the registrar by

responding passionately to the caresses of his boss.
It wasn't fair on Paul Tester, of course, and as soon
as his strong hands moved sensuously over her
body, Anna cried halt.

Paul moved a little away from her as they sat in
his car. 'Sorry. I must have misread the signals,' he
said mildly, and she turned anguished eyes on him.

Nervously she traced the pattern on his tie, what
little she could see of it in the dusk, and began a
halting apology. 'I'm so sorry, Paul. I . . . I didn't
mean to lead you on,' she began, but he captured
her hands and squeezed them understandingly.

'You aren't leading me on, my dear. You're
enchanting me!' he said lightly. 'You call the tune,
my love. I won't rush you,' he promised, moving
back to his own seat and starting the engine.

Anna felt cheap as well as ashamed. He was so
kind and she had used him, trying to forget the man
she loved in the arms of another. She could not
forget Rick nor cease loving him, no matter how
hard she tried, and she knew it was wrong to
encourage Paul. But, having ensnared him, she
didn't know how to release him without hurting his
feelings.

Having to lie to her mother made her feel cheap
as well, but there seemed no alternative. After
baring her soul about Mike Forster, Anna hoped
she and her mother might reach a closer understanding, that Mother would realise it was natural
for a young woman to want the company of men,
want to go out with a group too, dancing or ram-
bling or party-going. But Jennifer was withdrawing
into herself again, her demands becoming impossible to meet.

After much heart-searching Anna decided it was best to lead her own life as much as possible, leaving her Mother to draw her own conclusions about where her daughter went, and with whom. She didn't neglect her mother. She was as attentive as ever, but she tried harder to encourage her independence, though it was a losing battle.

She saw Mike Forster once more before he left for Northern Ireland. She kissed him for old times' sake and he clung to her, then astonished her by beginning to weep. Mike, the hard-bitten worldly boy from Liverpool, actually crying. Her heart bled for him and, hardly knowing what she was agreeing to, she promised to wait for him.

Of course he attempted to make love to her and in her pity for him Anna almost agreed. Only a picture of chilly, condemning blue-grey eyes prevented her in time. She could almost see the icy sparks flying from Rick Alexandre's eyes, even though he was on leave, presumably miles away in Jersey.

She could never belong to anyone but Rick. That fact was quite clear. Not even the urbane consultant had the power to stir her as Rick had done. All the Paul Testers and Mike Forsters in the world could not hold a candle to her dark Rickie Jerseyman.

As part of her campaign for getting out and about, Anna accepted a totally unexpected invitation to a leaving party. One of the girls in her set, Marion Burns, was discontinuing her training to get married. Her fiancé was an engineer and he was taking her abroad with him.

Anna got on well with Marion, a tall, lively

brunette of twenty or so, and she was looking forward to the party—anything to take her mind off the problem of having two men in tow, two men she did not want. She couldn't ask Dr Tester to accompany her to the party of course, that would have set the hospital tongues wagging!

She had finished promptly at five for once, but didn't leave the ward until nearly twenty past for Sister Noakes insisted she tidy the linen cupboard first. Then, when Sister inspected it, she wanted the sheets moved to another shelf and Anna, stifling a sigh, did as she was bid. Only one more day and she would be free of Sister Noakes, so she could put up with the woman's demands for that short while. On the whole Sister had not been too hard on her recently so Anna had good reason for believing that her ward report would be a fair one, showing her to be an average student, which was as much as anyone could hope for. She knew that much as she loved nursing, she wasn't a born nurse. She wasn't brilliant at studying either, despite being a boffin's daughter. But she tried hard and was genuinely fond of the patients and she hoped Sister would take that into account.

After eating a hurried tea then bathing and changing into a pretty white and gold dress, Anna made her way back to the hospital. The party was being held in the Nurses' Home common-room. Snuggling down into her jacket Anna was at first oblivious to the car which drove slowly past her. When it stopped, she quickened her pace, believing it was someone from the hospital waiting to offer her a lift.

It was. The driver got out and peered into the

darkness at Anna. In the light from the car head-lights it wasn't difficult to see who it was, and she checked her stride as Rick Alexandre opened the car door for her. Unwillingly, she got in. She'd wanted to refuse the lift but that would have been stupid and childish.

'Still strolling in the dark, then,' he commented as he put the car into gear.

'Yes.' Her voice was quiet, muffled because she was snuggled down into the warmth of her sheep-skin. She hoped he would take the hint and not press her to talk.

She heard his soft chuckle and her face burned with indignation. He was making fun of her again. But he respected her wish for silence, thank good-ness. She turned puzzled eyes on him as they walked side by side to the common-room. 'I didn't think senior registrars went to student nurses' par-ties,' she commented, and his wide shoulders lifted in a shrug.

'A party is a party. Lots of birds and booze,' he said mildly. Anna immediately thought of Beth Sinclair.

'What about your girlfriend? Couldn't she come?' She managed to keep her voice neutral, but the registrar shot her a quick glance.

'Which one? I haven't a regular girlfriend.'

'Oh? What about Beth—from the Path Lab,' she probed and he smiled, enigmatically.

'I can't take her to a party. What Beth and I do is best done in private!' he chuckled, and Anna drew in her breath sharply.

Well, she had asked so couldn't grumble. He had laid it on the line for her. He and Beth were lovers and she was most likely waiting for him at his bungalow.

Anna bit her lip savagely, all thoughts of the party gone from her. In fact, she didn't want to go to the party any more. Beth might be preparing Rick's supper at this very moment. The table would be set for two, the glasses and the cutlery sparkling, the cloth of crisp white linen. They would dine by candlelight, she decided. Then Rick would reach out and take Beth's hand, those long, sensitive fingers reaching for her . . .

'Hey! You've passed it!' Rick's amused voice brought Anna back to earth and she found that she had walked straight past the common-room, hadn't even heard the noise emanating from the party.

She heard it now, a blend of raucous music and loud voices. She couldn't face them. She really could not, but now Rick's hand was in hers, urging her into the room, where they were immediately brought into a circle of nurses including Marion, the party-giver.

After the eats and the talking, there was dancing to some old slow music records and Anna was half-glad, half-sorry. If Rick asked her to dance it would be sheer heaven and sheer hell at the same time.

But to her annoyance he did not ask her. He danced once with Marion, then duty having been done, he spent the rest of the evening talking to a couple of housemen who came late. Anna was left to her own devices and, after chatting briefly to the few people she knew, she made her way to the door.

She was nearly there when she felt a heavy hand on her shoulder. She turned, sharp retort at the ready, but it was one of the male nurses, not Rick at all. She smiled warmly at the nurse, whose name was Doug. She didn't know his surname or even what year he was, but she allowed herself to be swung into his arms. He was about her own height, with glossy black hair worn rather long and brown eyes. Quite handsome, too, she was thinking when Doug suddenly swung her to the side of the room, thanked her, then disappeared.

Amazed, Anna had no time to collect her thoughts before she saw Rick. He was holding out her jacket and obediently she slipped her arms into it.

'Stay there,' he ordered, making his way towards the engaged couple, presumably to say goodnight.

A surprised Anna stood where he'd left her, still wondering why Doug had ditched her in the middle of a dance. Then she saw him hovering nearby, and beckoned him over.

With a quick glance towards the registrar, whose back was to them, Doug came over and smiled ruefully. 'Sorry. You ought to have said.'

'Said what?' she asked, becoming more puzzled by the minute. 'You left me in the middle of a dance!' she went on.

'You should have said you belonged to Rickie Jerseyman,' Doug said patiently. 'That's why I brought you back to him. When we were dancing I saw him staring. Then he pointed at you, and at himself, so I gave in gracefully!' he laughed.

'I don't belong to any man!' she said sharply. 'He had no right to butt in!' She clenched her fists, ready for action, then saw Rick making his way determinedly towards them.

Doug saw him at the same time and did a quick disappearing act. It would have struck Anna as amusing if two other men and another girl had been involved, but as she was the girl in question it was far from funny.

She was determined to give the registrar a piece of her mind but he gave her no chance. Quickly they were out in the car-park and he was bending to unlock his car door. On the walk through the corridors he had strode ahead and she had had difficulty in keeping up with him.

Not that she wanted to keep up with him, of course. She had no intention of letting him drive her home, but she *was* going to tell Mr Rickie Jerseyman exactly what she thought of him.

'Come on, Anna. It's too cold to hang about.' With an impatient gesture he pushed her into the front seat.

'Look here,' she began, as he settled himself beside her.

Quizzical blue-grey eyes were turned towards her and he leaned forward until his face was mere inches from her own. 'Yes, Nurse?' he mocked, and Anna felt like slapping him.

But he was not the sort of man you slapped. She felt sure he would seek instant retribution, so she refrained. 'You had no right to tell Doug I belonged to you!' she stormed.

'Did I say that? I didn't, you know. I simply pointed to you and his imagination did the rest,' Rick said smugly.

'Well, you had no right!' she repeated, her voice cracked and strained. To her horror she felt a tear coursing down her cheek and she turned away from him, not wanting him to know she was crying.

'Anna?' His voice came hesitantly, then he gathered her into his arms and she lay there quietly, struggling to keep back the tears, but they came all the same.

'Anna, you aren't crying are you? Not my tough little girl,' he said tenderly, and she was suddenly still in his arms.

How sweet and gentle he sounded, how kind. Almost as if he cared about her. With a sigh she wormed her way out of his embrace, then fished in her bag for a hankie. 'Sorry. I'm just tired, I guess.' Her voice was faint but controlled now, and he made no further comment.

Not only did he take her right to her home, he drove between the stone entrance posts and right up to the front door.

When she thanked him stiffly for the lift, he ran his index finger down the side of her cheek and she quivered, believing he was going to kiss her. Her eyes closed, but he made no move towards her.

'On Saturday you can come to tea at my bungalow,' he said instead, and her eyes flickered open.

'To tea?' she echoed, wondering why. Surely Beth was available at weekends?

'Mm. I'm having a few people in,' he went on, and she fought down her disappointment. They were not to be alone then.

He made arrangements to pick her up directly after lunch on Saturday then saw her to the door, waiting while she inserted her key into the lock.

That she ought to refuse his invitation she already knew. He had a nerve expecting her to fill a gap when it suited him! Probably Beth Sinclair was away and that was why he'd asked her—no, *ordered* her—to have tea with him. No matter. She knew quite well she would go.

Anna felt obliged to tell her mother about the invitation to tea but Jennifer did not appear interested. She fixed reproachful eyes on Anna and pointed out that she'd been told the relationship was over. Apart from that no more was said, but Anna felt the disapproval wafting across to her.

If only there was some way she could shake Mother out of her apathy. Mother might as well be dead for all the enjoyment she was getting from life. She had, after all, perhaps another twenty or more years to live.

Anna hardly slept that night. On top of her worry about her mother there was the morning to be faced—the dreaded ward report.

She was right to dread the report. It was a bad one, and she let out an audible gasp as she read it in Sister's office the next morning.

Sister Noakes sat opposite Anna, head bent as she twiddled with the cap of her fountain pen.

'Surely I'm not *that* bad,' Anna said plaintively, and Sister looked up, her expression disapproving.

'You aren't exactly bad, Nurse Curtis. But you are not exactly good, either,' she commented, her eyes cold as they rested on Anna's bright hair. 'I have marked you as average on most things,' she pointed out, and Anna's voice shook as she retorted,

'Where I'm not average you've marked me as below. And your comments leave no room for doubt that I'm *well* below!' She almost choked on the words but Sister showed no signs of emotion as she reached across and took the report from Anna's trembling fingers.

Sister signed it then passed the pen across to Anna. The student had to sign that she'd read and understood the report, also that she'd had an opportunity to discuss it. Space was left for the student nurse to make any other comments she thought relevant, particularly if she disagreed with the report.

Well, this student certainly disagreed! Anna thought stormily, as she signed the report and added a few pungent comments.

Sister gave a grim smile after she'd read Anna's comments then thanked her for all her assistance during her spell on Park Ward. She probably meant it sarcastically but Anna chose to take the remark at face value and said how much she had enjoyed men's medical. That at least was true. She would miss the men, and most of the staff too, particularly Ruth Barratt who was the sort of woman Anna would have liked for her mother. Ruth was someone who listened to everyone's troubles, letting nurses and patients alike pour out their sorrows.

Just talking about one's problems with a neutral observer made a difference, and Anna had briefly told Ruth about Dr Tester's interest in her. The auxiliary had already noticed the amount of attention the consultant was paying Anna so the news came as no surprise. Her advice was to let matters ride for a time and see how the relationship developed. As long as she made it clear to Dr Tester that she desired only his friendship he would have no cause to complain when she rebuffed any passionate advances he might make.

Anna had a date with him that same evening. He'd had a busy day so for a change he took her to the ballet—where he slept through the entire performance. He was apologetic afterwards but it didn't matter. She had so enjoyed the ballet that she might have been alone in the theatre, she certainly had not missed Paul's company! When he kissed her as they parted, Anna repeated Ruth Barratt's words to him, and he gave a heavy sigh. 'Only my friendship? Is that all you want, Anna?'

Anna was sure of it and said so, and he sighed again. Her lips quirked. He was a bit like Mother, making the most of every dramatic situation. 'All right. Friendship it shall be.' He sounded defeated but she hardened her heart. From now on it was what Anna Curtis wanted that mattered!

CHAPTER TEN

As SATURDAY afternoon approached Anna became more and more nervous. Did she actually want to have tea with him? The answer to that question was never in doubt! She needed his company, needed to feast her eyes upon his dear face, needed to feel the force of those beautiful blue-grey eyes. Yes, she would go.

It was a free weekend for her. On Monday she started two weeks in the Nurses' Training School when the ward reports would be dissected under the stern eye of Mrs Lucas, the Principal Tutor. That would be an ordeal, more of an ordeal than meeting these friends of Rick's. After her two weeks study block she was due to go to the children's ward. She could hardly wait. Then she would do nights on the same ward, after which she would have her much-needed holiday. By then it would be late spring . . . No, she corrected herself, mentally counting off the weeks. She would start nights in the middle of May. Why, her holiday wouldn't be until June! Three and a half months to wait.

Neat in her green woollen dress, Anna sat by the study window waiting for Rick to arrive. June. Jersey would be nice in June. Not too crowded, with room to move. If only she and Rick could be together in Jersey! They would stroll along by one of the bays, gazing down at the sandy beach below. Everywhere there would be the scent of flowers.

Rick would smile into her eyes and rain soft kisses upon her face. The lines on his dear face would deepen as he laughed down at her. Then he would whisper tender words of love. The sun would shine out of a cloudless blue sky, with not a shower in sight . . .

Anna now realised what she had been gazing at for the last few minutes. Rain. Big spots of rain pattered against the window-pane, and sadly she watched them slide down the window to lose themselves where the glass ended and the sill began. Rain was all she needed! So much for day-dreams.

When Rick arrived she was in a foul temper, her mood matched only by the weather, the angry lowering sky, the bare, dripping trees. There was no point in going out with him. She could see no future in their relationship. It was painfully obvious that he preferred Beth Sinclair, so why not cut her losses and refuse to have anything more to do with him?

With one smile from Rick her good intentions vanished like the sun. No matter how little she got from the friendship, Anna knew she couldn't keep away from him. He was worth the agony and all the heartache she suffered. To belong to such a man would be the ultimate joy. But even to enjoy his friendship for a little while was better than nothing, she conceded.

Rick was casually dressed in dark cords and a wind-cheater, his checked shirt open at the neck, exposing the strong, masculine column of his throat.

Her arms ached for him and she wanted to brush back the tendril of black hair which hung tantalisingly over his brow. It was damp with the rain and curled ever so slightly. Anna was enchanted with it. She'd never realised that his hair had a slight curl. She bit her lip, turning away so that he should not see the eagerness in her eyes. He would chuckle to himself.

She allowed him to help her into her jacket and asked who his other guests were.

Rick didn't answer until she was safely in the front seat of his car. 'Just one or two people I know,' he said mysteriously and Anna sat back, annoyed both with him for not telling her and with herself for asking. She ought not to have betrayed her curiosity. It gave him an unfair advantage.

The pretty bungalow welcomed them. At least Anna was almost sure it did. She had a better chance to see it this time. On her previous visit heated emotions had come between her and admiring the scenery!

It seemed deserted and she stopped, feeling mulish. No way was she going in if they were to be alone. The passionate interlude of last time was still fresh in her memory.

He frowned, the lines deepening at the corners of his mouth. Obeying an impulse Anna put her fingers on his lips.

'Don't frown, Rick. You'll get lines and wrinkles.' His eyes widened in amazement and, shocked at her temerity, Anna snatched her hand away as if she'd touched a red-hot poker. 'I . . .' she floundered, then the door was opened and a tall, grey-haired woman smiled at them.

Rick's steely fingers just above her elbow denied

all resistance. Anna tried to return the woman's smile but could manage only a grimace.

The woman stared reprovingly at Rick. 'What *have* you been doing to the poor girl, Rick? I thought she wanted to come?'

Anna, mystified, began to protest that she *did* want to come, and the mystery was solved when Rick introduced them. The grey-haired woman was his mother. Anna smiled shyly, still baffled. Why he should want her to meet his mother she could not imagine, but no doubt there would be others present.

But the only other guest was Rick's father. When Anna met him she spotted the resemblance straight away, no one could doubt they were father and son. Rick resembled his mother not at all, but his father had similar blue-grey eyes, dark hair with not a trace of grey, and an upright, athletic build that many men half his age would have envied. In him Anna saw Rick at fifty-five or so, and her beaming smile left no doubt of her approval. Having one Rick around was heaven. Two of them was a bonus!

'Glad you approve, Anna.' Rick's voice in her ear made her jump and she coloured, wishing she had not appeared so enthusiastic. She must not get too friendly with his parents.

But it was hard not to be friendly with them, and Anna found herself half way through her life story before she realised. She broke off, discomfited. They must be bored to tears.

But his mother encouraged her to talk about her own mother, and Anna briefly mentioned the attack, the subsequent slow recovery, then Mother's lack of interest in living.

'It often happens, love,' Mrs Alexandre put in when Anna paused unhappily. 'We knew a woman just like that, didn't we, Fred? You remember Mrs Picot, don't you?'

Her husband smiled and nodded. His smile, the way it deepened the lines running from his nose to the corner of his mouth, was so much like Rick's that Anna had to lower her gaze, pretending an interest in the home-made rug under her feet.

Mrs Alexandre chatted on, and Anna smiled and nodded in what she hoped were appropriate places. Rick's parents were nice. They were so homely that it was a pleasure just to sit with them.

Rick was lucky to have parents like them and they were lucky to have a son like him. It brought home to her forcefully that she had no real family, only the memories of her beloved father to keep her going. She had always been more of a father's girl. Perhaps that was why she was unable to help her mother overcome her apathy, persuade her to get on with living. She would try harder, Anna vowed, try and not accept defeat.

'Admiring the rug, are you?' Rick's husky voice spoke from the doorway. He wheeled in a trolley of tea and cakes and Anna laughed. About his waist was a tiny lace apron, the sort waitresses sometimes wore.

A pained expression crossed his craggy face, then he grinned. 'Pretty, isn't it? I was Waitress of the Year once!' he quipped.

Apart from the cakes, there were neat little sandwiches, vol-au-vents, and an enormous gateau, rich with chocolate and cherries. A Black

Forest gateau! It was her favourite and she couldn't resist asking if Rick had made it.

'Him!' his mother said dryly, 'it will be a day when he makes anything! He can manage an omelette and that's it.'

'It's better than gateaux,' Rick pointed out. 'I could live on omelettes if I had to. Mother made it,' he went on, indicating the gateau.

'It's a hobby of mine,' Mrs Alexandre said. 'I make all the cakes for the guests.'

'Guests?' Anna looked blank.

'We run a guest-house. At Greve de Lecq. Didn't Rick tell you?' Mrs Alexandre gave her son a reproving look, and he smiled, unrepentant.

'When I'm with Anna we have other things to discuss, Mother. Other things to do, as well!' he said cheekily, knowing Anna would blush.

She did, of course, but his mother, seeing her embarrassment, began to talk about the guest-house run by her husband and herself. 'We don't open until Easter and we close in October as a rule, but if you're ever in Jersey do look us up. It doesn't matter if we are closed. We can always find a room for any friend of Rick's.'

Overwhelmed, Anna thanked her, believing she might take up the invitation. She would go late in the year, she decided, perhaps early October when she had another fortnight's holiday. She wouldn't wish to disturb them out of season.

All too soon dusk was upon them and Anna knew she must leave. Nurse Dixon was at home but Anna felt guilty at leaving her mother for so long. It wasn't fair. From under her long, gold-tipped lashes Anna surveyed the family scene before her.

Rick stood with his back to the fireplace, his face animated as he described a hospital colleague to his father, who sat contentedly puffing on a cigar. Mrs Alexandre began to clear away the dishes and Anna jumped up to help, glad to get away from the family circle. It brought home her own and her mother's isolation—and it hurt.

When Rick drove her back to Millstones, he left her with a cheery wave. He made no attempt to kiss her or even squeeze her hand, and perversely Anna was angry. She would have objected, or tried to, if he'd caressed her, but surely a little kiss wouldn't have hurt? One kiss from him was worth half a dozen from anyone else. It was hard to believe now that she had once enjoyed Mike Forster's caresses. Hard to believe she endured those of Paul Tester, as well.

Anna knew now, after that little glimpse of heaven, that she would rather stay in every night than spend even a minute with another man. Getting the message across to Dr Tester was hard, though. At first he didn't understand. When he did, he became angry, a vein standing out at the corner of his brow.

Anna feared for his blood pressure, but he didn't appreciate her concern and told her so, brusquely.

'I'm sorry,' she murmured. They were having dinner at a club not far from Southampton. As always, she'd insisted on going Dutch so that she would not be beholden to him. She stared down at her steak, her appetite gone, little nerves in her stomach jumping and fluttering about. She hated scenes, avoided people with quick tempers, but she had to be honest with him. It would do the man no good to keep on hoping.

'Am I to know the name of my successor?' he asked nastily, and Anna's eyes flashed. He put up a hand as if in surrender. 'Green fire, Anna. You'll never be poor while you have emeralds for eyes,' he said wryly, drawing back his chair, leaving the steak untouched in front of him.

'Well—who is he?' he demanded, as he obediently stopped his car several yards from her gate.

Anna dropped her eyes. 'No one in particular,' she said after a lengthy silence, and Paul laughed harshly.

'There is, but you aren't going to tell me,' he commented. 'I suppose, whoever he is, he doesn't know you exist?' Taking her silence for confirmation, he went on, 'The fellow must be blind. Anna Curtis carrying a torch for him and he doesn't notice!'

She moved to get out of the car, but he placed a hand on her shoulder. 'Anna!' he pleaded. 'I love you, I *need* you!'

'No. It was just friendship, remember? I suppose I was naive, thinking I could have a platonic friendship with you,' she whispered, hating herself for what she was doing to him, yet knowing it was in Paul's best interests.

Without another word he let her go, and a disconsolate Anna walked the remaining few yards to Millstones. If only love wasn't so complicated.

During the two weeks she was in school, Anna clung to the thought that Rick had wanted her to meet his parents. Surely that meant some degree of involvement on his part? He wouldn't take every girlfriend home to meet them. It was a comforting thought, but as she walked to the Training School at the end of her second week, she saw Beth Sinclair and Rick, hand in hand.

With eyes that ached because of her unshed tears, Anna watched them get into Rick's car. Beth laughed up at him, Anna could see her sparkling teeth even from that far away. Then the car turned out of the hospital driveway and sped away in the direction of the coast. Towards Rick's bungalow. Of course they might have been going for a drive, or . . . Or perhaps Rick was taking Beth to meet his parents before they returned to Jersey.

It was bitter gall to her. And, on top of that, she had an unpleasant interview with Mrs Lucas, who expressed her disappointment in Anna's report from Park Ward. Anna must, she said, show a marked improvement. The tutor uttered no threats, did not say 'or else' but the words were implied, and Anna was nearly in tears when she got home. From now on, she vowed, she would work and study until she dropped. Her career was of vital importance. Men were definitely out!

Anna managed to keep her resolution for a whole week. She was on the children's ward now—Summer Ward. It was full of noise from morning till night and she found it strange at first. Never having been used to children, the noise and chatter gave her a splitting headache, but by the time her days off came around, she was reluctant to leave the children. One of them, Jimmy, a boy of seven, was just like a junior version of Rick, and he became her special favourite.

Mothers were allowed to visit at any time they wished—indeed visiting hours were very generous throughout the hospital. Jimmy's mother had three other children, all younger than him, so could not visit very often, and Anna tried to give him extra attention, simply because he had no one else. She hated leaving him for her two days off, but promised to bring him a present when she returned.

She was browsing through the quaint Middleborough shops for Jimmy's gift when she bumped into Rick Alexandre. He, too, was examining toys and putting them down again.

'It's been a long time, Anna. How is your love-life?' he asked softly, beginning to turn the key of a mechanical rabbit.

A sad-eyed Anna ignored the remark and watched the rabbit perform its jerky dance, emitting squeaks as it turned. 'I don't like that,' Rick commented, but Anna was making her way to the soft toy counter. Why should Rick care about her love-life? She *had* no love-life without him, so it was a waste of time replying.

What on earth did one buy for a boy of seven? Spoilt for choice she eventually settled on some drawing books and non-toxic pens, knowing how children loved to suck pens and pencils. She would give the pens to him when he was being discharged. Sister wouldn't thank her for brightly coloured sheets!

Rick wandered over and waved a furry duck at her. 'Like this? Or shall I buy a teddy?'

'What? Oh, a teddy is so ordinary. Everyone has a teddy bear!'

'I haven't. Never mind, what about this pink

elephant? He's really handsome,' Rick enthused, and Anna tried to forget her heartache in helping him find a suitable cuddly toy—presumably for a nephew or niece. Niece, she decided, as he finally bought the pink elephant. His mother had told her that Rick's married sister often helped in the guest-house.

'I'm off tomorrow,' he said suddenly, and Anna gave him a suspicious look.

'That's nice for you,' she said tartly, then wished she hadn't as his face darkened. 'Forgive me, Rick. I'm just overtired,' she murmured, trying to hide her resentment. He turned to her only when no one better was available. It was so obvious—surely he must realise she knew? Perhaps he thought she was so besotted with him that she was content to be second-best. In a way that was true, but she didn't intend him to find out!

'Children's ward getting you down, is it?'

Her green eyes softened. 'No, I love it. But the noise was hard to take at first. Then the mothers are always around. When they're chatting among themselves it doesn't help!'

'I like kids. I want three of my own. Or four. Have to see how it goes!' he joked, and Anna felt sick.

It was probably mingled jealousy and shock rather than anything serious, but she knew she had to sit down. Wildly she gazed around for a chair or the exit. Fresh air. That was what she needed.

With a muttered excuse she thrust the books and pens into Rick's arms and dashed out, not stopping until she was outside the little store. There were several benches nearby and she plonked herself down on one. It was too cold to sit about but she was glad of the support for her legs.

Whatever must Rick be thinking? He would believe her mad. But it was his fault she felt ill! Boasting about the children he and that . . . that Beth Sinclair were going to have! Quite likely they'd started one already. The more she thought about it, the more truth there seemed to be in her wild guess. Beth hadn't looked well when Anna saw her in the canteen a couple of days before. The 'flu epidemic was over, so . . .

Rick's baby. A baby boy, with large blue-grey eyes and . . . Anna almost choked as she forced back the tears. It could be that the fluffy elephant was for his baby. She must be pleased for them both, must not begrudge Rick a little happiness. True love meant that you wished your loved one happiness, even if he could not be happy with you. If it *was* true love she felt for Rick then she must be glad for him. Glad. She clenched her fists, then Rick was beside her, stroking her cold, numb fingers back into life.

From out of the depths of her misery Anna summoned up a sweet smile for him. He must never know that he had just trodden on her heart. 'I'm sorry. I felt rather sick,' she explained, and he dropped her hands as if he'd touched a hot brick.

'Too much studying, I expect,' he said brusquely, leading her towards his car. 'Or too many late nights,' he added.

'No. I'm always in early,' she protested. 'Really there's no need to give me a lift.'

He stopped so suddenly that a passer-by bumped

into them. Waiting until the man had gone, he snapped, 'Why? Is he picking you up?' The blue-grey eyes were sending out storm signals and Anna was half afraid of the anger she saw there.

'No one is picking me up,' she said stubbornly. 'I . . . Oh! I meant those books and pens for little Jimmy! I'll have to go back.' A package was thrust into her hands and she stared at it stupidly.

'It's the books and pens,' Rick explained slowly, as if she really was stupid. 'The books and pens you threw at me when you felt . . . unwell.'

Before she could thank him, he was gone, and Anna was left standing in the middle of the High Street, her gift clutched to her chest. The man she loved strolled away without a backward glance.

'But she was all right when I left her!' Anna could not believe that her mother had suffered another heart attack, and her mind went blank, shutting out the shrill tones of Nurse Dixon, who had tele-phoned her on Summer Ward. 'She can't have. She . . .' Anna stopped, realisation dawning at last. Mother was seriously ill and she must hurry home. If only she didn't feel so inadequate!

As she flung her raincoat on, Anna wondered why Nurse Dixon hadn't requested an ambu-lance—perhaps it was already too late . . . Wishing she had listened more carefully to the phone mes-sage she hurried along the corridor, longing for the sight of Rick's familiar figure. *He* would under-stand, would help. But children's ward was a long way off his beat. The only way she could contact him was by having him bleeped, and she didn't dare. It wasn't his problem. In any case, Mother's doctor would probably be there by the time she arrived.

Fear lent wings to her feet as she began the mad dash across the car-park. She hadn't waited to call a taxi, knowing she could be home before it arrived. She was nearly at the hospital entrance when a car tooted behind her. Could it be Rick? Her lips half formed his name as she spun round—to meet the baffled gaze of Paul Tester.

'Oh, Paul! Could you give me a lift?' she pleaded, feeling bad at using him but her mother's needs were paramount.

Without a word he opened the door and she collapsed against him, panting. 'I feel awful asking you, but . . . it's Mother!' she burst out, filling him in on the details as they drove.

'Might it be hysterical?' he queried, frowning. They drew up outside the house before Anna could answer, and she was upset that Dr Smith's car wasn't there.

'He hasn't come! Poor Mother!' Without waiting for the consultant, Anna dashed in through the open front door then paused uncertainly. She could hear raised voices and she thought the noise came from her mother's room.

She put her finger to her lips as she tiptoed towards the room, followed by Paul, who muttered that her mother was surprisingly vocal for a person who was at death's door.

Anna shot him a pained glance and his lips quirked. Embarrassed and angry because she had panicked when she ought to have remained calm, Anna softly opened the door.

Jennifer was lying back against umpteen pillows,

spots of colour on her cheeks, kneading a large handkerchief, her hands moving restlessly. Nurse Dixon raised an eyebrow at Anna, then pursed her lips and shrugged.

Anna knew that meant Jennifer was giving a performance and that she hadn't been in real danger. Relieved, she ran towards her mother, flinging her arms around the taut, tearful figure.

'Mother! You had me so worried!' she scolded, then remembered to her horror that she'd brought a consultant out on a wild-goose chase!

Paul Tester hovered in the doorway, looking puzzled. Then his face cleared and he and Jennifer stared at each other. Perplexed, Anna looked from one to the other, expecting to see anger on the doctor's face. Instead his expression was indefinable. Amazement, disbelief and some other emotion were mingled on his heavy features. It was her mother who broke the silence.

'Paul? Paul Tester! It *is* you?' Jennifer disentangled herself from Anna, and opened her arms in welcome to the consultant.

Anna moved aside as Paul was enfolded in her mother's embrace. That certainly was unexpected! She wasn't sure she liked another woman enjoying Paul's caresses even if the woman *was* her mother, but she shrugged aside her unease. Paul must be an old friend and if meeting him gave Mother the incentive to live, it was well worth it.

To Anna's embarrassment, Jennifer lifted her face to be kissed and, after a moment's hesitation, Paul kissed her gently on the lips. Then his eyes met Anna's and they exchanged sad smiles. Even if their romance hadn't been at an end before it must be ended now. For Jennifer's sake they must resume their professional relationship.

Jennifer's eyes darted anxiously from one to the other. 'How did you come to bring Paul, darling?' she asked Anna, her voice querulous. 'He and I were great friends once.'

'I was dashing home and when I saw P . . . Dr Tester's car,' Anna faltered, 'I begged a lift. I thought you unwell,' she went on sternly, and Jennifer lowered her eyes coyly.

'I'm in disgrace, Paul. Tell my little girl not to scold me!'

'I'm afraid I agree with her, Jenny,' Paul said sternly, getting up. 'She has her job to do. Patients rely on their nurses. They are probably short-staffed on children's as it is,' he went on, frowning at Jennifer, who still clutched at his hand.

'I will call and see you again, Jenny, but I'm just on my way to a conference—in Birmingham,' he added, as Jennifer would have detained him further. Ashen-faced, she watched as he and Anna walked out of the room.

Anna could still feel her mother's eyes boring into her back as she let the consultant out. When she began to apologise both for her mother's hysterics and her own panic, Paul brushed the words aside. Then, with a quick glance around to see that they were not overlooked, he swept Anna into his arms, his mouth hot yet curiously comforting upon her own.

For a moment she responded, then her mother's needs blocked out her own. Mother *needed* Paul. Anna did not. Mother had so little and must not be denied Paul's friendship, even if he wasn't keen on the idea.

'I want you, Anna,' he murmured, as she made him release her. She shook her head wearily, seeing him at last for what he was.

'You don't want *me*, Paul. You want your lost youth and I can't help you regain that.' Sadly, her eyes met his and she saw the truth there.

Angry spots of colour burned in his cheeks as he moved away, and Anna closed the door softly, feeling that she was closing a chapter of her life.

Jennifer was eager to talk about Paul Tester for days afterwards, telling Anna that he had been her boyfriend before she had even met Anna's father. Even then he had been fond of women, and Jennifer had reluctantly settled for security with a rather humdrum young man—Anna's father.

'Father wasn't humdrum!' Anna protested, and Jennifer smiled.

'No, but I thought he was. So serious! I was a bit flighty at first, I suppose. I was still acting then,' she explained. 'But I settled down once you came along. Your father was the best husband anyone could wish for. He was rather cold, poor dear. That was his only fault,' Jennifer went on, seemingly far away in thought.

'I shouldn't suppose Dr Tester is,' Anna said unthinkingly, and her mother's eyes narrowed suspiciously.

'Do you know him well?' she asked, her eyes on her daughter's face, and Anna cursed herself for mentioning the man.

'No, not well. He was the consultant on Park

Ward—Rick Alexandre's boss,' Anna said hurriedly.

'Yes, with that lovely hair, I suppose he *would* notice you,' Jennifer said pensively, settling down and demanding to be left alone as she wished to sleep.

After that, Jennifer did not mention Paul Tester again and she sank back once more into her apathetic state.

Watching her mother's almost lifeless figure one evening after she'd read to her, Anna knew what she must do. Reluctant suitor or not, Paul Tester must be persuaded to visit Mother again.

She hadn't seen Paul since the day he'd given her a lift. He might still be in Birmingham, as she hadn't seen him about the hospital, but it was worth a try.

The consultant's house was ablaze with lights when Anna hesitated outside it the following evening. Well, he was in, but who was he entertaining? If he had a woman friend in, it would be too embarrassing. And suppose he wouldn't come?

In an agony of indecision Anna pressed the bell. She hoped he would answer straight away, otherwise her courage might desert her and she would run.

Only the memory of her mother's sad eyes reminded Anna of her duty. No matter how nasty Paul was, she must stand her ground and beg him to visit.

CHAPTER ELEVEN

'ANNA! This *is* a surprise.' Paul Tester's voice was far from welcoming and Anna wished anew that she hadn't come. The old manservant who let her in wore a disapproving expression, and she guessed he was tired of the constant stream of women visiting his master.

They stood in the box-like hall, Paul not even offering her a seat, and Anna twisted her signet-ring nervously. If only he didn't look so angry.

'Well?' he barked, and she jumped.

'Please, Paul—it's Mother. She's ever so down now. Couldn't you just visit her? Only occasionally. It wouldn't be a bother to you, would it?' Anna hurried on, feeling wretched. How she hated to beg!

And the consultant wasn't helping her. He brushed back his hair with an impatient gesture. 'Look, Anna dear, once your mother and I were . . . friends, but that was *years* ago! And she doesn't seem any more mature now than she was then!' he added, and Anna silently agreed.

'Please, Paul. Please. Just a few minutes once a week—for old times' sake. Only until she begins living again. Your visit cheered her up enormously,' Anna assured him, her green eyes intense, and he capitulated.

'I'll come. Tomorrow, if I can. But right now I have guests and . . .'

Anna nodded quickly. He was obviously entertaining a girlfriend and Anna's presence was an
embarrassment. She smiled her thanks, and Paul
put out his hand in a gesture of friendship. Then he
pulled her towards him when she moved nearer to
shake hands.

With a sigh, she leant against his shoulder, his
arms about her. It was comforting . . .

'Sorry, chief,' a familiar voice broke up the cosy
scene as Rick Alexandre appeared in the doorway.
'I didn't know you were expecting a friend,' his cold
eyes raked over Anna, who stood her ground
defiantly.

'That's quite all right, Rick,' Paul said wearily.
'I'll do as you ask, Nurse Curtis. But it won't be
easy,' he went on, with a wry smile. Then he turned
to the bristling registrar. 'You could drop Nurse
Curtis off, couldn't you? She came in a taxi, but
they aren't easily come by at this time of night.'

Anna and the consultant waited for Rick's decision.

He shrugged. 'Of course, sir. Anything to
oblige.' His tone made it clear that it was his boss he
was obliging not Anna, and she felt about an inch
high.

Nevertheless, a lift was a lift and it was evident
that Paul wasn't going to drive her home. Perhaps
he needed to prepare himself for a second meeting
with Mother.

'What is St Paul doing for you?' Rick asked
sullenly, as his big car purred along. 'You were
thanking him most enthusiastically when I butted
in!'

'I can't tell you.' Anna felt the consultant would

want to keep his former relationship with Jennifer secret. Anyway it wasn't Rick's business. It concerned her mother and Paul Tester, no one else.

Rick grunted and Anna wished she *could* tell him. It wouldn't do any harm, surely? He wasn't a gossip. He would keep the information to himself. Anna sat back, relaxing, all tension ebbing from her. She could trust Rick. She would confide in him once they got home. She would ask him to pop in to see her mother, then she wouldn't wonder where Anna had been so late.

'Here we are. Safe and sound,' Rick announced, and Anna smiled into his eyes.

A stifled groan escaped him, then he sat back and she was left to open the car door herself. 'Will you come in, Rick? Have a coffee? Mother would be . . .'

'Yes, yes, all right,' he snapped, and Anna's temper rose. If he was going to be so mule-headed she wouldn't tell him about Paul Tester and her mother.

In a daze she followed him out of the car—then realised the sound in the background was the murmur of the sea. They were outside Rick's home, not hers! 'Rick?' she queried softly, but he ignored her as he unlocked his front door, and urged her inside.

The bungalow was warm but in darkness. Anna supposed his parents had returned to Jersey, 'Rick?' she said again. 'Please take me home— Mother will be so worried!'

'Doesn't it worry her that you sleep with a man old enough to be your father?' Rick barked, snapping on the lights and banging the front door.

'I don't!' Anna gasped, her eyes flashing. 'Surely you don't believe that?'

In the artificial light Rick looked haggard, weary. That lock of hair was getting in his eyes again but Anna resisted the impulse to push it back. In his present unpredictable mood anything might happen.

'I don't know what I believe any more,' he said, his voice tired. 'I thought you were a sweet, old-fashioned girl. Then I hear on the grapevine that you're out until all hours with that . . . that wolf! You went to see him this evening asking him a favour. You wouldn't dare ask a consultant for favours unless you were already giving him yours!' he snapped, and Anna flinched away from the contempt in his eyes.

'No, Rick! It wasn't like that! He and . . .' Anna began but was given no time to complete the sentence, to explain about her mother. Strong fingers closed on her wrist and she was half dragged towards a closed door. Panic-stricken, Anna struggled but could not prise her wrist free.

The closed door led to the bedroom. Anna's frightened gaze took in only the bareness of the room—and the size of the bed. Then Rick picked her up and laid her on the huge bed, his body following her.

'Rick! No!' she gasped, getting a hand free and raking her nails down the side of his face.

He swore, then captured both her hands so that she was left with teeth as her only defence, her legs crushed under the weight of him. Blood showed on the ugly scratch marks she'd made, and Anna stopped struggling. She'd hurt him!

'My poor Rick!' she murmured and, surprised, Rick let go of her hands. He flinched away as her right hand traced the marks she had made. 'Oh, Rick, I'm so sorry! I'll give you first aid,' she said determinedly, but Rick forced her down again.

'If I want first aid, I'm perfectly capable of giving it to myself!' he ground out, his eyes a stormy grey now. 'Does it turn you on to have a registrar as well as a consultant in your bed?' he went on, and Anna wished she'd scratched him harder. 'Maybe Paul and I should work out a rota!' he went on harshly, and Anna almost spat in her anger.

'What about you then? You and that . . . that Beth Sinclair!' she stormed, wishing she wasn't at such a disadvantage. Pinned to the bed as she was, it was difficult to quarrel.

'Beth? What about her?' Rick rolled on to his back, releasing Anna, who sat up, eyes sparking fire at him.

'You have so many girlfriends that I suppose *you* must have a rota! There's Beth Sinclair, and . . .' She paused uncertainly. *Did* he have others?

'Yes, Nurse?' Rick prompted her, his even breathing suggesting he was half-asleep.

How could he lie there so calmly. 'There's Margaret Warwick,' she went on.

Rick raised himself on one elbow and smiled. 'Margaret Warwick. Am I enjoying an affair with her as well?' he asked softly, his eyes no longer angry. Anna swallowed and moved further away from him.

She sat right on the edge of the bed, and heard his husky chuckle. 'She seemed fond of you,' she said stubbornly, and he chuckled again.

'Most women are fond of me,' he acknowledged smugly. 'I have lots of endearing little ways.'

Anna choked. 'I want to go home.'

'All right,' he said, surprising her. He rolled off the bed and stood gazing down at her. 'Just tell me one thing. Are you and Paul Tester having an affair?'

Anna's eyes met his. If she had seen tenderness there, or humour, she might have told him about her mother and Paul. But all she saw was bleakness, a remoteness in his gaze. He didn't care one way or the other. He was simply satisfying his curiosity. Well, she would not give him that satisfaction!

She shrugged. 'Mind your own business!' she retorted, and was momentarily afraid as Rick glared down at her, his fists clenching and unclenching at his sides.

He spun on his heel without another word, and Anna, her heart aching, watched his broad back disappear. From the sound of crockery being clashed, she gathered he was in the kitchen, and she followed him, her stockinged feet making no sound.

Unnoticed, she watched him making coffee, his strong, deft hands moving to and fro, his jaw set in a stubborn line. How she loved him! Her fingers ached to run themselves through his fine hair. She longed to smooth away the lines of temper and fatigue on his lean face. Longed, too, to feel his arms about her.

But it was a complete stranger who spun round at some sound she made. A tall, dark stranger, with bitterness etched on his face, with cold greyish eyes, his mouth a thin hard line, and Anna sighed for what she'd lost. He believed she was having an affair with his boss. Because of that, he despised her. She couldn't let him go on believing that, she couldn't!

'Rick,' she began, as he returned to his task. There was no sign that he'd even heard her, and resentfully, she tried again. 'Rick, do listen! I'm not . . That is, he and I aren't having an affair.'

'Oh?' He sounded uninterested, and Anna wanted to shake him. He could be so stubborn! He handed her a cup of black coffee and she stared down at it.

'If you want milk help yourself.' He pointed to a bottle on the table, and Anna's smile broke out.

'No jug?' she asked, helping herself to a spoonful of brown sugar and a little of the milk.

He shrugged. 'I'm not much good at looking after myself. At the hospital I generally eat in the canteen. Have my coffee there, too. Saves washing-up.'

Anna was surprised that Beth Sinclair didn't volunteer to char for him but wisely kept quiet. They drank their coffee in silence, then she tried again to explain about Paul Tester. 'He's an old friend of Mother's. She knew him before she met my father. I went there tonight to ask him to visit her again. No, to *beg* him to visit. Last time he came, he cheered Mother up,' she said earnestly, her eyes begging him to understand.

Rick looked unconvinced. 'In between times he cheers daughter up, I suppose.' he snapped, and Anna refused to say any more.

He didn't care! He wanted to believe the worst of

her. She hated him! 'I hate you, Rick Alexandre,' she said softly, the very quietness of her tone giving the words power.

'Good. I hate lying, cheating little bitches, too,' he said, equally softly. 'We know where we are now, don't we?'

In silence he drove her home. She was tempted to ask why he'd taken her to his own home but assumed it had been for a passionate interlude. If he genuinely believed she was the consultant's mistress, then he felt he had cause for grievance when she refused his own advances. Anna could see that clearly enough. That was the trouble. She could see Rick's point of view as clearly as her own, and that made it difficult to quarrel with him. He felt aggrieved and quite rightly so, from his viewpoint.

He opened the door for her to alight, and Anna made one final attempt to get this pig-headed man to see sense.

'Won't you come in to see Mother? She could tell you about Paul,' she pleaded.

'I'm sure you could tell me *all* about Paul, so why bother your mother?' He put the car into gear and moved off, leaving a desperately unhappy Anna to watch until the tail-lights disappeared from view.

Somehow, time passed for Anna. Her ward work kept her fully occupied and reasonably happy. Sister Kelmer was middle-aged and motherly, a favourite with staff as well as children. She always took an interest in staff problems and Anna had seen the Sister's sharp blue eyes on her more than once.

Another three weeks and her stint on Summer Ward would be over. Then she would do a month of night-duty on the ward. That might be rather fun, she mused, as she gently washed one of the newer patients, Gail Honeysett. A thin, pale child of six, Gail was in for a routine tonsillectomy. She'd had the operation the previous day but still hadn't rallied around the way children usually did.

Children were resilient, Anna found, quickly bouncing back after illnesses that would floor many adults. It occurred to her that Gail didn't *want* to get better because she didn't want to go home. She was an only child and in hospital she had lots of company. Her mother, an over-fussy woman in her late thirties, had brought her in but hadn't been since, and Anna didn't think Gail particularly missed her.

'Still keeping busy, then?' Sister Kelmer's soft Irish brogue interrupted Anna's thoughts.

'There's never a dull moment on your ward, Sister!' Anna laughed. Then she dropped a kiss on Gail's brow, and, gently disentangling herself from the girl's clinging hands she followed Sister to the office, wondering what she had done.

Probably Sister wanted an informal chat, or to do some teaching. Despite the heavy work-load, she was keen to give her students as much study-time as possible.

'I see Paul Tester keeps hanging around you in the canteen,' Sister said bluntly, after Anna had seated herself as requested.

'Oh? Does he?' He was always speaking to her in the canteen, even sitting at her table instead of with his own colleagues, and it was bound to cause comment. 'He talks about my mother,' Anna went on, and Sister shot her a sharp glance.

'Friends, are they? I thought he fancied you, and I wanted to warn you!' Sister said, with a wry smile.

Anna relaxed. 'Thank you, but I already know Dr Tester's reputation. He and Mother are old friends.' She was reluctant to say more, not even daring to hope that they might become more than friends. Paul still seemed to prefer her, but gradually the old Jennifer Curtis was emerging and Anna felt her mother was captivating Paul Tester all over again. She certainly hoped so. Her nerves wouldn't stand another Jenny Curtis relapse!

That evening Paul was a dinner guest and, as always now, Anna kept very much in the background, trying to merge with the surroundings as much as possible. To keep attention away from herself she wore a navy dress, and merely flicked a brush through her curls. Her mother scintillated in rich emerald green, her happy animated face making her a different woman from the one who, a few short weeks before, had wanted to die.

Nurse Dixon was still employed but now filled the role of companion more than nurse, and Anna was glad for her.

Jennifer and Paul linked hands at the end of the meal and Anna gazed uncertainly from one to the other. 'Paul and I are getting married next month!' her mother burst out excitedly.

'That's wonderful!' Anna rushed to embrace her mother but contented herself with giving her prospective stepfather a warm smile. 'Will you live here? I suppose you won't.' Anna answered her own question, and Jennifer cast her eyes down, while the consultant explained gently that he would be taking Jennifer to live with him.

'Your mother wants to sell Millstones,' he hurried on, avoiding Anna's direct gaze.

'Yes, naturally,' Anna murmured, thinking ruefully that the freedom for which she had so often longed was now within her grasp—and she had no use for it! No man of her own, no one to care for, no one to care about her. She had nothing, and her mother, it seemed, wasn't at all bothered.

'You must have a share of the proceeds, of course,' Jennifer put in quickly. 'Paul and I thought we might set you up in a flat of your own. Then you can visit us. Well, occasionally,' she added, and Anna knew her mother would never really trust her with Paul. Knowing Paul's weaknesses, she considered Mother had some cause for suspicion.

It was arranged that while Jennifer and Paul were on honeymoon—a quiet few days in Devon—Anna would move into the Nurses' Home.

It would solve all her transport problems, Anna reflected, walking to work the next day. She was on late shift and had left the house earlier than necessary to book her next driving lesson. She hadn't had many lessons, having lost interest in the idea of having a car, but if she was to be truly independent, she really ought to have one.

She stopped as she was about to enter the driving school office. A short, muscular figure with dark, crinkly hair was talking to the receptionist. Even as she watched, startled, Mike Forster kissed the girl then waved as he moved to the door.

Mike Forster—here in Middleborough! He was supposed to be working in the Belfast factory, gaining experience so he could be promoted once he returned home. There must be something wrong. Had he been shot?

All sorts of frightening thoughts flooded through Anna's brain as they came face to face outside.

Mike went brick-red. 'H . . . How are you, Anna?' he blurted out, his hand already reaching for a cigarette.

'I'm fine. How was Northern Ireland?' she asked sharply. Mike spent so long trying to light his cigarette that she thought he wasn't going to answer.

'It fell through!' The words didn't ring true, but Anna let it go. 'Then I lost my job, didn't I? Had to get another one. I've been on the dole, Anna. Honest! And I couldn't ask you to support me.' His pale eyes didn't meet hers.

'If you needed help, I wouldn't have turned you away,' she said patiently. 'Is Patty a friend of yours? I thought she was a newly-wed,' she went on curiously, knowing the receptionist, a pert blonde, had recently returned from her honeymoon.

'Er, yes. Friend of my mother's. Look, Anna,' he said, taking her arm and leading her away from the driving school. 'Couldn't we pick up where we left off?' he wheedled. 'You promised to wait for me.'

'You haven't been away,' she pointed out coldly. 'And you appear to be doing all right without any help from me.' She pulled her arm free and hurried along the High Street, her errand forgotten.

Mike didn't need her. Mother and Paul didn't need her. And most certainly Rick Alexandre didn't need her! She was alone again, more so now. Having loved and lost she could never regain her independence. She could never be free of Rick Alexandre even if their paths never crossed again.

As for Mike's duplicity—the receptionist's name was Patty Forster now, and Anna would have taken bets that her new husband's Christian name was Mike! No wonder he hadn't come to her when he needed money. He had a wife to support him.

Northern Ireland indeed! Promotion to assistant area manager. Mike had never intended to go. It was all a ruse to get her into his bed. When it failed he took whoever was willing. Anna smiled grimly. At least Patty had stood out for marriage. Perhaps she would help him grow up, where she herself had failed.

Anna sat, numb and silent, during the short flight to Jersey. She was still numb when the taxi dropped her outside the Alexandres' guest-house.

It was larger than she'd supposed, a big brick building standing back from the road just within sight of the sea. The term guest-house conjured up visions of half a dozen bedrooms and one bathroom, but this looked more like a private hotel.

Even now she couldn't believe her own temerity. Why had she come? What had possessed her to foist herself off on Rick's people? She hadn't even booked. Easter was past so the guest-house would be open—but even this early in the year it might be full.

Anna glanced up at the windows, trying to estimate how many bedrooms there might be. Ten? Fifteen? Supposing there was no room? No matter, she could ask.

The receptionist assumed her there was room but

only until Saturday. After that it would be house full, she explained.

Glad to have a room at all, Anna followed her upstairs, her overnight bag clutched firmly to her side. Oh, why had she come? Rick wouldn't be there. She'd seen him in the canteen the day before she'd left. Here she was in Jersey while he was across the sea! It didn't make sense.

But Anna knew why she'd come. Here, in his parents' home, she felt close to him. Once his parents knew she was here they would talk to her about Rick, tell her something of his childhood perhaps. She could never have Rick. He simply wasn't interested. But she would have her memories, and collect more knowledge of him to pore over on the long, cold evenings of her life.

It would be the following morning before she could see Mrs Alexandre. The receptionist told her the owners were in St Helier, the capital, on business. In the meantime, Anna strolled along the bay, breathing in the fresh, salty air. There were flowers everywhere, a riot of colour wherever she looked. She felt free, truly at one with the seascape.

Jennifer and Paul were marrying the next week. Millstones was up for sale but there were no buyers in view, and Anna had decided to stay on there until it was sold. She didn't really want to live in one pokey room in the Nurses' Home, not after having a whole house to roam through. Time enough for that after her home was sold. She might take up her mother's suggestion of a flat. There were several old houses divided into flats just off Middleborough High Street.

On her stroll she passed people who were

obviously honeymooners. A couple of about her own age, arms entwined, oblivious to anyone else. They stopped to kiss, and Anna nearly bumped into them. With a hollow feeling inside, she apologised, then hurried back to the guest-house. She ought not to have come. She'd forgotten that Jersey was a popular venue with honeymoon couples. There were two such couples staying with the Alexandres and it made her own heartache that much worse.

She had only three days there, having begged Sister Kelmer for three off duty days together. After the shock of her mother's engagement and proof of Mike Forster's two-timing, she felt she simply *had* to escape.

Mrs Alexandre was delighted to see Anna the next day and equally delighted to talk about her only son.

'Rick never said you were coming! Are you comfortable, Anna? Is your room all right?' Rick's mother fussed around her like a real mother, and poor Anna could hold back her grief no longer.

The whole sad story came tumbling out, including Rick's disbelieving her story about her mother and the consultant. Mrs Alexandre stroked Anna's hair, murmuring soft, consoling words, and to her shame she fell asleep on the settee in his mother's private sitting-room, her head resting on the woman's ample bosom. Months of bottling up her troubles had taken their toll. Anna needed deep, refreshing sleep, freedom from worry, and a chance to unburden herself. All these she found in Jersey.

They treated her more like family than a guest.

Rick's father even drove her into St Helier, a bustling sea-port, on her last morning so she could buy some souvenirs. It wouldn't do to visit Jersey and not take home her duty-frees!

For her mother she chose a bottle of French perfume. She hesitated over something for Paul. It would be a small wedding gift for him so her mother could hardly object. She'd already chosen their main wedding present, a bone china tea and dinner service. Mother had china of her own and so had Paul, but they were both delighted with the set. Something new for their new life together, as Jennifer had put it.

In the end she didn't buy Paul anything. It was better that way. What they'd shared together was in the past, and there was no point in upsetting Mother unnecessarily.

Whilst in St Helier, Anna took the opportunity of following the tourist route, as far as her time allowed. She strolled across Royal Square, pausing for a while to enjoy the late spring sunshine. It was warmer there than at home. She joined the crowds doing their duty-free shopping, and ate an enormous ice-cream while she watched the tourists stroll. She had no time to visit Fort Regent, or the castle, but was determined to return to the island one day for a much longer visit.

After the crowded town, she was glad to get back to the peace of Greve de Lecq. She sighed, thinking that it was the perfect spot for a honeymoon.

Her footprints in the sand looked lonely. One pair of prints where there might have been two. Tears pricked her eyelids as she said goodbye to Greve de Lecq, goodbye to Jersey. Then she cheered up a little as she remembered the souvenirs she had to take with her—memories of a warm welcome, little snippets about Rick from her mother, and, most important of all, a photograph of him taken the summer before. Mrs Alexandre had pressed the photo on Anna, assuring her that Rick would be returning to Jersey in the autumn and that she could get one for herself then. It was the best memento Anna could have, and she told Rick's mother she would treasure it always.

The flight home was over almost as soon as it began and Anna's faint hopes of a joyful reunion with Rick faded away. She had half hoped his mother might have telephoned the hospital and begged her son to come home. It was a foolish dream and bore no resemblance to reality. Rick couldn't leave his work just like that. Nor was he likely to rush over to Jersey just to see a girl he could see every day at St Aidan's. It was only a daydream and the sooner she settled back in her routine, the better.

Mrs Jenkins fussed over Anna when she returned. The Jersey sun had brought colour to her cheeks, and she felt fitter, better able to cope with her mother now. But once Mrs Jenkins had bustled away to make tea she saw it wasn't her mother who glared at Anna from the armchair in her father's study—it was Rick Alexandre!

Before she could compose herself, he strode over and shook her. 'Why in heaven's name did you go traipsing off to Jersey? I was out of my mind with worry until Mother phoned!' he snapped, then gathered her into his arms, smoothing back her curls with one hand. With the other he tilted her chin. 'Oh, Anna! How can I live with you? How can I live without you is more to the point!' he continued, with a smile.

Anna's green eyes widened uncertainly. With this man she never really knew anything. No woman could ever be sure of Rick. He was like quicksilver. One minute you had him, the next he had slipped through your fingers. 'Did you miss me then? I thought I was Paul Tester's property, not yours,' she said testily.

He groaned. 'Anna, I never believed that. I wanted to, all the evidence pointed that way, yet . . . I hoped you had more sense. Fancy turning me down and taking him! No woman could be that stupid!' he chuckled, and she raised her lips for his kiss.

'I did think you might be pregnant. That day you were buying toys in Middleborough,' he added reluctantly, and Anna gasped. 'I know, I know,' he soothed, 'but you felt sick and I . . .'

'That was because you said you wanted children!' she interrupted. 'I had visions of Beth Sinclair bearing your children, and I was sick with jealousy!'

He chuckled, then drew her close again. 'Beth filled a need. She was good fun but I always wanted you. I still want you, Anna. I want you and I intend to marry you, so let's have no arguments!' he went on firmly. Anna gave her sad-sweet smile.

Want but not love. No word of love. But it didn't matter. She had love enough in her heart for both of them. She returned his kiss, warm and content in his arms.

By mutual consent they refused the housekeeper's offer of tea and sped away in his car to his little bungalow.

There Anna finally found out what it was like to be a woman. She had no qualms, no fears such as she'd experienced at the thought of Mike's love-making. She put her hope and her trust into Rick's safe-keeping, along with her heart, body, and soul, and she was richly rewarded.

This was love. Heaven itself could offer no more. Only one shadow marred the sunshine. Rick still did not, even in the heat of passion, utter one word of love. Anna knew it shouldn't matter but it did.

He'd made love to her, taken all she had to offer, but was it simply a physical need on his part, she wondered, half asleep in his arms.

Then the telephone shrilled. 'Hell! Duty calls, I expect.' Rick, tall and beautiful in his nakedness, shot out of bed, and held a hurried conversation with what she took to be a colleague. 'Yes, all right. I'll be there in twenty minutes,' he sighed, thumping down the receiver.

Anna smiled sadly, then opened her arms to him, reluctant to let him go. He evaded her arms, merely dropping a kiss on her brow.

'Get dressed quickly and I'll drop you off at Millstones on my way back.'

A tired but happy Anna got out of the car outside her home and prepared to wave Rick off. Her cup of happiness would be full—if only he loved her!

As he drove away, his lips formed the words 'I love you'.

She waved until he was out of sight. Rick did love her! Rick loves me, Rick loves me, she chanted to herself as she went indoors. She had given herself in the name of love and had no more fears for the future.

Jersey would be just the place for their honeymoon, she thought dreamily, as she closed the door.